Kathleen's Abiding Hope

Kathleen's Abiding Hope

BOOK THREE

of the

A Life of Faith: Kathleen McKenzie

Series

TRACY LEININGER CRAVEN

Franklin, Tennessee

Book Three of the *A Life of Faith: Kathleen McKenzie* Series

Kathleen's Abiding Hope

Published by Mission City Press, Inc.

Cover & Interior Design: Richmond & Williams
Typesetting: BookSetters

For more information, write to Mission City Press at 202 Second Avenue South, Franklin, Tennessee 37064, or visit our Web Site at:

www.alifeoffaith.com

Library of Congress Catalog Card Number: 2006930442
Craven, Tracy Leininger
Kathleen's Abiding Hope
Book Three of the *A Life of Faith: Kathleen McKenzie* Series
ISBN-13: 978-1-928749-27-1
ISBN-10: 1-928749-27-5

Printed in the United States of America
4 5 6 7 8 — 11 10 09

DEDICATION

To my husband, David, for his unfailing love and support and to our precious daughter Elaina Hope.

Telephone Systems in the 1930s

The phone system in use during the 1930s was unlike our telephones today. Phones in those days were powered by batteries. When an individual wanted to make a call, he or she would pick up their telephone line and reach the operator, who sat in front of one to three banks of phone jacks. She would then connect their line to the number requested. In rural areas of the country, phone lines were connected to "party lines" in order to have service in less populated areas. This meant that neighbors shared a phone line. If you wanted to make a call, it was never completely private; people could pick up the telephone in their home and listen to your conversation on the shared line.

Feed and Flour Sack Dresses

During the Depression era, people learned to be creative with their limited resources. The saying "Waste not, want not" held true during that period in history when individuals placed value on those things we often take for granted. One of the most creative, money-saving ideas was the use of flower and feed sacks for fabric. Resourceful mothers could make everything from dresses and swimming suits to bedsheets and quilts from flour and feed sacks. The feed sacks were made of cotton material, not like the burlap or heavy paper sacks we think of today. When purchasing chicken feed, the main questions were which feed was best for the chickens, and which fabric was best suited for the desired new shirt, dress, apron, or curtains. Flour sacks were made of a finer weave and were usually white. This made for very nice bloomers and dish towels.

Road Conditions and Speed Limits in the 1930s

Road conditions in the 1930s were very different from the interstate and highway systems we are familiar with in our modern era. It was not until 1930 that the federal government set a minimum age for driving and established the requirement that all vehicles be insured. The Road Traffic Act of 1934 introduced a speed limit of 30 miles per hour in "built-up" areas. Rural farm roads were not paved and were often filled with potholes and washed-out areas that presented unforeseen travel difficulties. Therefore, it took much longer to arrive at an intended destination, especially in wet or icy weather.

McKenzie Family Tree

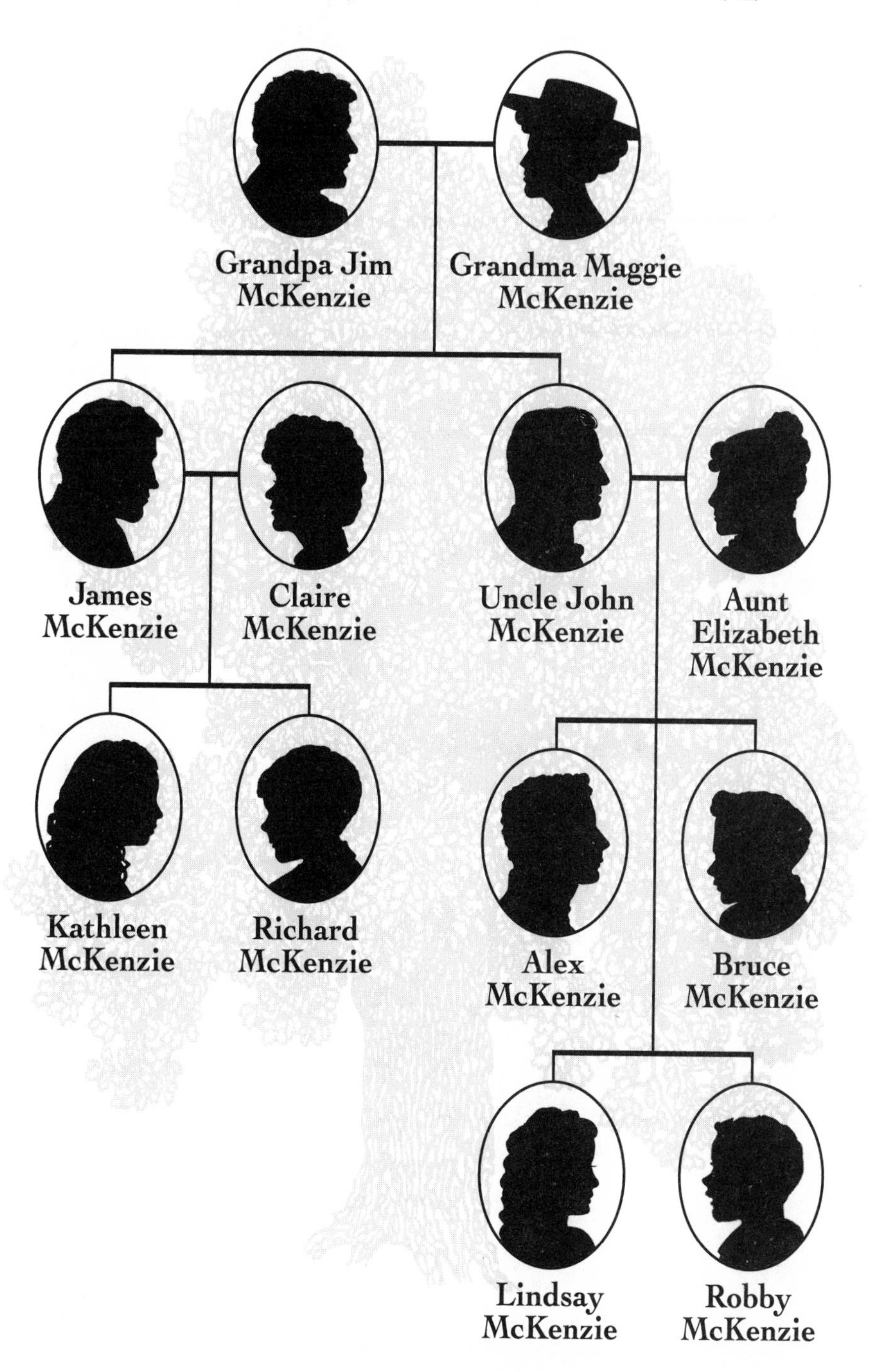

SETTING

The story continues during the winter of 1930. Kathleen and her family live with relatives at Stonehaven, the McKenzie family farm in Ohio, while her father finds employment. Kathleen has just received news that her best friend in Fort Wayne, Indiana, has been gravely ill.

CHARACTERS

THE MCKENZIE HOUSEHOLD

James McKenzie—Age 35, Kathleen's father
Claire McKenzie—Age 32, Kathleen's mother
Their children:
Kathleen McKenzie—Age 12
Richard McKenzie—Age 9

Grandma Maggie and Grandpa Jim McKenzie—Kathleen's grandparents
Aunt Elizabeth and Uncle John McKenzie—Kathleen's aunt and uncle, and their children:
Alex—Age 18, Kathleen's cousin
Bruce—Age 15, Kathleen's cousin
Lindsay—Age 14, Kathleen's cousin
Robby—Age 8, Kathleen's cousin

OTHERS

Lucy Meier—Age 12, Kathleen's best friend in Fort Wayne, Indiana
Peter Meier—Age 14, Lucy's brother

Dr. and Mrs. Schmitt—Family doctor and his wife, friends of the McKenzies and parents of:

> **Freddie Schmitt**—Schoolmate and friend of Kathleen

Mr. and Mrs. Johnston—Neighbors and owner of the dog Old Bruiser, and suspected members of the Ku Klux Klan

Mr. and Mrs. Williams—The McKenzie family's new neighbors that just moved to Ohio farm country from the South, and parents of:

> **Sharly**—Age 13
> **Emma**—Age 10
> **Elias**—Age 8
> **Tara Lee**—Age 6
> **Sammy**—Age 3
> **Earl**—Age 8 months

Pastor and Mrs. Scott—The McKenzie family's Ohio pastor and his wife, and their son:

> **William**—Age 16

Sheriff Ratcliff—Archbold, Ohio, town sheriff

Mr. Willaby Wallace—owner of Wallace Gas and General Store

CHAPTER 1

Devastating News

You will keep in perfect peace him whose mind is steadfast, because he trusts in you. Trust in the LORD forever, for the LORD, the LORD, is the Rock eternal.

ISAIAH 26:3–4

Kathleen's heart beat wildly as she opened the letter from her friend Freddie Schmitt. It had been written two weeks before, but she didn't care. Freddie's note was the first communication she had received since moving to her grandparents' farm in Ohio, and Kathleen was anxious to hear news from her friends back home in Fort Wayne, Indiana. The letter brought the devastating report of Lucy's illness. Kathleen's hands shook with fear. Her best friend's life was in danger. Lucy had already been ill with pneumonia just a few months before, and Kathleen feared that another bout of the sickness would be deadly.

"Dear God, please let me see Lucy again," Kathleen whispered. "You know her lungs are weak. Lord, give her the strength to pull through again. Freddie says that Dr. Schmitt sent for her brother—that means Lucy must be dangerously ill . . ." Kathleen's voice trembled as she prayed. She opened her eyes and stared at the letter that had slipped from her fingers and dropped to the floor. A hot tear ran down her cheek.

Candlelight danced against the wall and across the floor of her cousin Lindsay's room. Moments before it had looked so warm and cheerful. Now, with the news about Lucy, the room grew dismal. The long, shifting shadows seemed menacing and foreboding. Kathleen felt as though she were trapped in a dark dungeon—trapped far, far away from the sickbed of her most beloved friend. This feeling intensified as she looked out the window at the seemingly endless sea of frozen farmland and realized there was nothing she could do. There was no electricity and not even a telephone at Stonehaven Farm.

Since moving here, that had not been a problem; she'd gotten used to cooking on a wood-burning stove, using an outhouse, and reading by candlelight, but now, if only they had a telephone . . .

"I don't *have* to see her, Lord," Kathleen whispered. "If I could just hear her voice and know she is fine." She picked up her doll, Marguerite, which her

parents had given Kathleen on her twelfth birthday, and straightened the doll's dress. Lucy and she had so many wonderful memories of playing with their dolls together. Kathleen thought of last summer, and the fun times they spent together, making curtains for the tree house that Papa had built, doing homework, and having tea parties. Kathleen sighed; if only she could get back to Fort Wayne.

But wait! Earlier in the evening her papa had told her he planned to leave the next morning for Fort Wayne in search of a job. The news of Lucy's grim illness had made her forget.

Kathleen brushed a wisp of light red hair out of her face with shaking fingers. She placed Marguerite carefully back on the bed and jumped to her feet.

Her cousin Lindsay opened the bedroom door. By now Kathleen had become used to a lot of things about life on the farm, but she still wasn't used to sharing a room with her cousin.

"Is everything okay?" Lindsay asked. Her face was flush from sitting in front of the fireplace in the living room. "You've been up here a long time; I was beginning to worry."

Kathleen quickly told her about her letter from Freddie and her plan to see Lucy. "Surely my papa won't mind if I go along when I tell him about Lucy."

"What about school?" Lindsay asked. "We've already missed one week because of the blizzard, and

you said you didn't want to get behind. What will your papa say about that?"

Kathleen knew her cousin was right. Her papa wouldn't want her to miss any more school. An idea came to her. "I could bring my books and work twice as hard to make up my lessons."

Lindsay thrust her hands into her worn overall pockets and shook her head, making her blonde braids swing. "I sure couldn't do that. It's hard enough for me to focus on my books at school."

"I know it's going to be hard, but I need to see Lucy and know that she's okay." Kathleen headed downstairs in search of Papa.

~

"Papa, how long will it take to drive to Fort Wayne?" Kathleen pressed her face against the frosted car window and tried to make out familiar roadside landmarks in the dim morning light. All she saw were fields covered in snow.

"Well, lass, we've been driving for about twenty minutes—I figure with the roads as icy as they are, it will be early this afternoon before we pull into our driveway." James McKenzie glanced tenderly at his daughter and ran his finger down her freckled cheek and lifted her chin. "Keep your spirits up, my little princess. God willing, you will be at Lucy's bedside this very evening."

Kathleen nervously ran her hand across the smooth, white leather seat and tried hard to smile at Papa, but her stomach was all tied up in knots and her heart ached. The uncertainty of not knowing the seriousness of Lucy's sickness was unbearable. "My heart could rest easier if only I knew how she is doing." Kathleen's eyes filled with tears as they often had since last night after she had read Freddie's letter. "I'm trying not to fret but . . . Papa, my schoolmate Mary died last winter of pneumonia—the very same thing. What if Lucy doesn't pull through either . . . or, what if . . . if Lucy has alrea—?" Kathleen's voice tightened and a sob welled up in her throat, making it impossible for her to finish her sentence.

Papa took his right hand off the steering wheel and patted her knee. "There now, Kathleen, let's not think of that now. I know this life of ours is fleeting—but I do think we should hope and pray for the best. And in the meantime, try not to let your fears get the better of you. Lucy is one of God's children, and I know He will take care of her." Papa's voice was gentle and comforting.

"I know He will. I also know H-Heaven is a wonderful place. But if . . . if God decided to take her there . . . I would m-miss her miserably. She has become my best friend in the entire world. I really don't know what I'd do w-without her. The worst news would be better than this awful feeling of not knowing a s-single thing," Kathleen managed to say through her sobs.

"There now, Kathleen." Papa pulled her over next to him and put his arm around her. "I know how you feel—it's understandable and totally natural. It's good for you to speak what's on your mind. Take heart, my bonnie lass. We need to stop at the next gas station to fuel up. I think I can spare a few pennies for a telephone call to the Meiers' house." Papa grinned.

"Papa, do we really have enough money to make a phone call?" Kathleen leaned over and wiped the frost from the window and peered out, hoping to see something besides miles of rolling, snow-covered farmland. Surely there was a town nearby—or at least a filling station.

"I'll have more than a few pennies to spare if all goes well with my job interview—but until then, we can spare some money for something as important as this."

Kathleen could scarcely wait until they reached the next town. Finally she spotted a sign that read "Bryan, Fifteen Miles Ahead." The country road was in terrible condition with deep ruts and potholes. Kathleen knew that with the road conditions as they were, it would take forever to reach the outskirts of that town. It was still early morning and the sun had not risen high enough to melt the ice off the roads, and Papa was driving carefully on the slick, rutted

roads. Just when Kathleen thought she could not wait another minute, she sighted another sign.

" 'Rinner's Gas and General Store, Two Miles Ahead'! " shouted Kathleen, as she read the sign. "They should have a phone, don't you think, Papa?"

"I would expect they would, lass," Papa answered, his eyes on the road.

Dear Lord, please be with Lucy and help her to get better. And Lord, when I do speak with the Meiers, please give me the strength to bear the news . . . whatever it may be, Kathleen prayed.

As they pulled into the gas station, Kathleen's heart filled with dread. The idea of walking into the store, making the phone call, and possibly hearing terribly bad news about Lucy was more than she could stand.

Papa must have seen the fear on her face. "I'll call, Kathleen—that is, if you would prefer. It might be best if I spoke with Mr. Meier."

Kathleen felt a wave of relief. "Yes, thank you, Papa. I—I just couldn't face—"

"No need to explain, lass. I'd be nervous too."

Kathleen watched gratefully as her papa wrapped his black wool coat and scarf tightly around his broad frame and quickly ran up the wooden steps of the general store. She was thankful to have a father like him. Her papa was one in a million—no, he was better than that, he was the greatest man she had ever known.

Moments later, a lad who did not look much older than Kathleen rushed out of the building and began pumping gasoline into the tank. Kathleen scarcely noticed. All she could think about was the telephone conversation that was taking place inside the weathered general store. In her nervousness, Kathleen ran her fingers up and down the lining of her thick, red coat. The minutes dragged as she watched the entrance. At first Kathleen thought the worst news would be better than not knowing anything, but now she had her doubts.

"Dear Lord, please give me courage," Kathleen prayed. When she opened her eyes, Papa was walking back toward the car. She searched his face for a sign of what he had found out about her dear friend. His look appeared blank—almost expressionless.

"No one answered the telephone, Kathleen," Papa said as he climbed in the car. "I'm sorry. It looks like we'll have to wait until the next stop before we know anything."

Kathleen felt like the day he'd announced they were moving to Ohio, confused, disbelieving, and nervous all at the same time. What did this mean? Why wasn't there anyone at the house?

"I did get you a little something to tempt your appetite." Papa pulled out a brown paper bag from his coat pocket and produced a root beer candy cane. "I know it isn't much, but I thought . . ."

"Oh! Papa." Kathleen tried her hardest to sound cheerful. "That was so thoughtful—you know how I love root beer candy canes! I haven't had one in ages." She was truly grateful, but Kathleen had not eaten a bite of food since she'd read the news of Lucy's illness, and unfortunately, she still did not have the slightest appetite. However, for Papa's sake, she would try to eat it.

Papa put the key in the ignition, started the car, and drove back out onto the icy road.

Kathleen gazed out the window and sucked on the long candy cane with the white and brown stripes, but her mind was far away. She remembered the first time she'd met Lucy. It had been at the Highland Games and they had both been running in the same race. Kathleen had known even then there was something special about her. The only reason Lucy had run that race was for her brother, Peter. And when she and Kathleen crashed, Lucy's first thought had not been for herself, but for Kathleen. It didn't seem right that someone so kind and giving was so ill.

Suddenly Kathleen remembered that her Grandma Maggie had slipped a letter into her coat pocket earlier that morning as she gave her a hug good-bye.

"Don't open it now—it's just a little something for ye to think on during your long journey. God be with you, lassie . . . and remember, you're one of His precious lambs, so He is always with you."

Kathleen eagerly plunged her hand into her pocket. She knew that whatever Grandma Maggie wrote would be worth reading. She seemed to know exactly what to say when Kathleen was going through a hard time. In fact, sometimes Grandma Maggie did not even need to say a word. Kathleen could just see in her eyes that she understood and she cared. Of course, she'd been through far more trials in her lifetime than Kathleen could even begin to imagine. Grandma Maggie would always say, "I wouldn't trade my life experiences for anything—the trials are what God used to draw me closer to my Savior. They are what shaped me into who I am today." Kathleen knew that if God could make something beautiful and loving out of Grandma Maggie's difficult childhood, then He could heal Lucy too.

Kathleen unfolded the letter and gently smoothed the paper with her hand. It read:

Dear Kathleen,

These verses have often been a comfort to me no matter how difficult the trial. Just keep your eyes focused on your Heavenly Father, trusting that He is in control, and His peace will dwell in your heart.

"You will keep in perfect peace him whose mind is steadfast, because he trusts in you. Trust in the LORD forever, for the LORD, the LORD, is the Rock eternal." (Isaiah 26:3–4)

I am praying for you and for your friend Lucy.

Love,
Grandma Maggie

Kathleen read the verse several times until she could recite it from memory. Gradually, she began to understand what the words meant.

"You"—that must be God—"will keep in perfect peace him whose mind is steadfast." That must mean my heart will be at peace if my mind is steadfast—fixed or focused—on the Lord. "Trust in the Lord forever, for the Lord, the Lord, is the Rock eternal." That means that if I trust in God, He will be my everlasting strength!

"Papa!" Kathleen broke the silence. "I've been asking God to take care of Lucy, but I haven't been praying with a heart full of faith. Instead my mind and heart have been full of worries and doubts." Kathleen's words ran together as she scarcely took time to draw breath.

Papa glanced at her, a smile on his face. "Why don't we pray for Lucy right now, lass, and you can ask God to help you trust Him as you feel you should." He put his hand on Kathleen's knee and gave it a little squeeze.

"Yes, thank you, Papa. I think that would be best." Kathleen closed her eyes and bowed her head.

"Dear God, please help me to trust You fully," Kathleen prayed earnestly. "Lord, I want to fix my eyes on You and trust You to care for Lucy. Lord, You are the Great Physician—and You know what is best. Dear Father, I give Lucy to You—please heal her if that be Your will. But most of all, help me to trust You and help me to walk in Your peace. Amen."

"There lass, how does your heart feel now? Has your Heavenly Father lifted the burden?" Papa asked.

Kathleen opened her eyes. It was not that she suddenly had lost her concern for Lucy, or even that she felt confident that God would heal her friend, but deep within her heart Kathleen felt an unexplainable peace.

"Yes, Papa, I am peaceful—my heart trusts the Lord for His best." Kathleen took a deep breath and sighed. It was a relief to trust Jesus with the deepest cares of her heart. A yawn escaped from her mouth, and she realized how sleepy she was. She closed her eyes and before long drifted into a deep sleep.

CHAPTER 2

Mr. Willaby Wallace

The Lord your God is with you, he is mighty to save. He will take great delight in you, he will quiet you with his love, he will rejoice over you with singing.

ZEPHANIAH 3:17

The next several hours passed quickly. Kathleen found that talking with Papa made the trip go faster. She was still eager to hear how Lucy was doing, but deep within her heart there was an abiding hope that God was tenderly holding her friend in the palm of His hand.

"What do you think the county schoolhouse will be like, Papa?" Kathleen asked, her thoughts turning to the fact that she would miss yet another week of school. First, it was the long blizzard that hindered her from attending the local one-room schoolhouse; now it was the trip to Fort Wayne and Lucy's illness.

That didn't matter to Kathleen. She was keeping her studies up on her own, especially English, literature, and spelling. Kathleen still held on to the hope of competing in the National Spelling Bee that spring in Washington, D.C. Though Papa had not spoken of it, Kathleen knew that the last glimmer of hope for her to compete in it hinged on his job interview.

"It was a fine school when I was a senior there seventeen years ago—that is why I turned out to be so bright." Papa turned his attention from the road and winked at her.

"You mean you went there?"

"I sure did, lass. The community hasn't grown much since I was a boy. I guess they haven't needed a bigger building."

Kathleen still could not believe that she would be attending a school with all the grades combined in one room. It seemed so ancient—like something she had read in a history book about the pioneer days.

"Papa, I know that there isn't a large chance that I will be able to attend the National Spelling Bee in a couple of months—but . . . well, do you think that it will be a possibility if you get the job with this . . . what kind of company is it?" Kathleen asked. She knew it would be a big expense to travel all the way to Washington, D.C., and she should not have her heart set on it, but try as she might, she could not help dreaming about the possibility. She'd looked up pictures of the capital in a book at the library, and ever since she'd wanted to see the Lincoln Memorial, the Capitol Building, and especially the White House.

"It is a sales position with a company that sells life insurance," Papa said slowly. "If I get this job . . . we *might* have enough money for the journey, but it is not likely." He took his eyes off the road and looked at her intently. "Kathleen, you need to be prepared. Jobs are hard to come by—I have no guarantee that I'll get this one." His attention returned to his driving.

The thought of not being able to go to Washington, D.C. was painful, but not as much as it had been in the past. Kathleen was surprised. Maybe with everything that had happened and now with Lucy being sick—the National Spelling Bee did not seem as important as it once did. Despite what might happen with Papa's job interview, Kathleen knew she could be grateful for the health that God had blessed her and her family with. She had rarely been sick a day in her life—now that was something to be thankful for.

Papa reached into his pocket, pulled out his pocket watch, and glanced down at it. "It is near lunchtime—I don't know about you, lass," he said, putting it away, "but I'm getting mighty hungry for those sandwiches your mama packed." Papa patted his stomach.

"I'm hungry, too. Do you suppose we can call the Meiers' house when we stop?" Kathleen scanned the gray, overcast horizon for any sign of a town.

"I could not enjoy my lunch until we did." Papa pointed at a sign. "Let's see, Fairview is just ten miles ahead. We'll stop there."

Kathleen gazed out the window at the rolling fields, dotted every so often with a lonely farmhouse and barn. It had not snowed as much in this area as it had back at the family farm. She was glad to actually see patches of dirt in the field instead of endless snow. Kathleen's thoughts were mainly focused on calling Lucy's family to find out how she was faring. Whenever fear threatened to well up in her heart, she closed her eyes, asked God for strength, and then repeated the verse Grandma Maggie had given to her.

Before long, they pulled into a run-down gas station at the edge of town. Papa must have noticed Kathleen's questioning look, for he said, "It is not the nicest looking establishment, but the price of gas is the cheapest I've seen this entire trip."

"Maybe it's nicer inside." Kathleen eyed the one rusted pump that sat out front of an old, unpainted wooden building that tilted to one side and looked as if it might topple over with the slightest puff of wind. "Are you sure it's open? It doesn't look like anyone has used this building in years."

Papa chuckled. "The appearance isn't very convincing, but the sign hanging on the door says "Wallace Gas and General, Open: Please Come In," and there is smoke coming out of the rusted stovepipe on the roof. At least we know it will be warm. Let's go see if they have a telephone and a place to sit so we can eat our lunch."

Kathleen followed closely behind her papa as he walked up the snow-packed steps and opened the creaky door with rusted hinges. It once had been painted white, but now most of the color had chipped away. Inside, Kathleen was surprised to find a small, cozy room. At the far end of it sat a potbellied stove with a small table and a couple of chairs nearby. The cash register counter stood at the opposite side nearer to the door they had just entered. Lining the walls were large cotton sacks filled with various grains and feed for livestock. Kathleen had seen similar sacks in the barn at Stonehaven. Above them were shelves packed with smaller bags of flour, sugar, and rolled oats, several baking powder tins, and buckets of candy. Hanging from the ceiling were various farm and kitchen supplies—wash buckets, pitchforks, horse blankets, and even handmade straw brooms. Behind the cash register were shelves loaded with general pharmaceuticals and toiletry items. Despite its small, unkempt appearance from the outside, this store had everything imaginable inside. Most important, Kathleen spied a phone mounted on the wall behind the register counter.

"Welcome to my establishment. Will it be gasoline for you, sir, or is there something else that I might interest you in?" asked a small, squeaky voice from somewhere in the vicinity of the cash register.

Kathleen did not see who was talking. Then she saw a red tuft of hair rising from the other side of the tall counter. Next, a pair of hands grabbed the barstool seat. Abruptly, the shopkeeper popped up from behind the cash register, startling Kathleen and making her jump. For a brief moment, she stared in disbelief. There before her sat a person who was the size of a child but with the face of a grown man. He wore a miniature black business suit that offset his blazing red hair, which was balding in a perfect circle at the top of his head.

"Why, thank you," said Papa. "Gasoline and a phone call are our most pressing needs."

"You'll have to pump it yourself—our gas prices are the cheapest in the county, but you have to work for it." The small man waved at the pump outside.

"That works just fine for me. I do have one favor to ask of you. After our phone call and after I pump the gas, would you mind if my daughter and I eat our packed lunch at your table?" Papa asked.

The man leaned over the tall counter and looked at Kathleen. "Sorry, I didn't notice you, miss. Guess you've never seen one like me, but I'm a real live midget."

Kathleen blushed deeply; she didn't mean for her face to display such obvious surprise. "I'm sorry, sir; it is just that—"

"You don't need to apologize. Folks used to bother me with their gawks and unashamed stares, but not anymore. Many great men throughout history were short in stature. Napoleon, for example, was short, but his stature did not stop him from accomplishing great things. In fact, there are many advantages in my height. For instance, I can fit in more places than most people." He abruptly turned to Papa. "The phone is two cents for local calls and eight for long distance. I may charge more than most folks, but I'll let you talk as long as you wish—within reason that is, within reason."

Kathleen gazed up at Papa anxiously; eight cents was a lot for a phone call. Papa reached into his pocket, produced a dime, and plunked it down on the counter without flinching. "We'd like to make a call to Fort Wayne, Indiana."

The little man turned around on the seat, stood on his tiptoes, picked up the phone, and dialed the operator. Despite the growing anxiety for her friend, Kathleen stared in wonder at this unique

person who, talkative as he was, had not told them his name. She admired his positive outlook on life and outgoing personality. The whole situation—the old, leaning building that seemed cold and unwelcoming on the outside but was warm and cozy on the inside, the red-headed midget with the small, squeaky voice, who looked like a jester in a king's palace of old, but had a heart as bold and strong as King Richard the Lionhearted—it all seemed like a scene in a medieval play or a make-believe novel. She could hardly wait to tell Lucy all about it.

The little man handed her father the phone. "Yes, operator, could you please connect me with Peter Meier's home, Ivy Lane, Fort Wayne, Indiana. Thank you." Papa gave her an encouraging glance as he waited for the call to go through.

Kathleen hoped someone would answer this time.

"Good afternoon. This is James McKenzie. Is Mr. Meier available?" There was a pause and Kathleen fidgeted with a button on her coat. They were home. *Dear God, let Lucy be all right.*

Finally, Papa spoke. "Yes, I'd be happy to wait." Papa cupped his hand over the receiver and looked down at Kathleen. "I didn't recognize the voice, but they sounded in good spirits."

Kathleen remembered that Freddie's letter said Lucy's brother, Peter, had been called home because of her illness. Would he have answered the phone?

"Of course," Papa added, "you never can tell, but we'll hope it means the best."

Kathleen nodded her head and sighed deeply.

Please, Lord, does this mean she is better? Please help me to keep my mind stayed on You.

CHAPTER

3

Word of Lucy

For it is God who works in you to will and to act according to his good purpose.

PHILIPPIANS 2:13

Kathleen looked up at Papa, phone receiver pressed to his ear, and held her breath as she waited to hear how Lucy was doing. What was taking so long?

"Hello, Mr. Meier? I am calling to see how Lucy is doing. We received word through Freddie Schmitt that she was ill." Kathleen listened to her papa's steady voice and admired his ability to be so calm at such a time. If she were speaking, Kathleen was sure her voice would shake with nervousness. Kathleen was anxious to know what her papa was hearing on the other end of the line—or even to catch his eye for some sort of assurance. His brow furrowed with concern. What did that mean?

Finally, he nodded his head in agreement and replied, "Yes, I understand fully. I see how you would have been deeply concerned—and must still be. Praise the Lord that she seems to be on the mend. Kathleen has been beside herself to find out how Lucy is faring. Freddie must have written when Lucy was in the most danger." Papa turned and smiled down at Kathleen.

The relief on his face washed through her like a healing balm. Lucy was okay. A big smile broke out on Kathleen's face.

"Is it a friend or relative that your pop's checking up on?" the little man whispered, trying not to interrupt the phone conversation.

"Lucy is my best friend. She has come down with a severe case of pneumonia and until now, I wasn't sure if she had pulled through or not. It looks like God has answered—"

Papa's voice broke her sentence. "Yes, yes—that would be good. Kathleen and I are heading to town and I know my daughter won't sleep a wink until she sees Lucy tonight. Are you sure it's okay? We don't want to disobey the doctor's orders."

Kathleen could not believe what she was hearing. She would be able to see Lucy that very night. Tears of gratefulness welled up in Kathleen's eyes, and she clasped her hands together. "God is so good! I gave Lucy to Him, trusting His best, and He has answered my prayers."

The little man behind the counter frowned and shook his head.

Kathleen wondered at his response but was too overcome with joy to pay much attention. As soon as Papa hung up the phone, Kathleen threw her arms around his neck in a big hug.

Papa picked Kathleen up and twirled her around in a circle. "Lucy is on the mend, lass. She's not completely out of danger, but things are looking up. God has answered our prayers."

"Oh, Papa! Tell me everything! Is Peter still there? Did I hear you right? Do I really get to visit Lucy tonight?"

Papa gently brushed the curl from Kathleen's face, a constant problem that her stubborn cowlick created. "Now this is the lively Kathleen I'm used to being with. I was wondering when she would return. Tell you what. I'll answer all your questions after I fill up the car with gasoline. Why don't you set our lunch on the table and I'll be back in a jiffy," Papa said as he turned to go out the door.

Kathleen almost forgot about the shopkeeper on the other side of the counter until she heard some faint muttering. She looked in his direction and saw him shaking his head and murmuring something under his breath in obvious displeasure.

"I'm sorry, what did you say?" she asked.

He waved his hand. "You and your father. It's easy to believe there is a God when everything works out the way you want it to. Just wait, miss. When life treats you a little harder, you might not find it as easy to trust that there is an all-loving God."

At first Kathleen was offended at his statement. She wanted to defend herself and express the trials that her family had been through the last several months with Papa being out of a job and having to move to Stonehaven Farm. But then she felt a tugging in her heart. A thought came to her that she had not considered. She knew God had a plan in all these events. Maybe the Lord had brought them all the way to this unusual place just to tell the shopkeeper about His grace and love.

Heavenly Father, help me to be an example of faith and trust in You to this shopkeeper. Please bless this man, Lord, and help him to see Your love and peace reflected in our lives.

Kathleen smiled at the man behind the counter and replied calmly, "You're right, sir. It's easier to trust God when everything works out the way you want. The real test of faith comes when things don't work out the way you planned." Kathleen walked over to the table at the far end of the room next to the potbellied stove. "I do pray that I will be able to exhibit the same level of faith in the difficult times. For instance, I won the Indiana statewide spelling bee and should

be going to nationals in Washington, D.C. this spring."

"Congratulations, little lady—your response regarding your faith was evidence enough that you have a sharp brain inside that pretty little head, but now I *know* you're smart," the man said from his bar-stool perch.

"Thank you," Kathleen said as she blushed.

"I wish you the best of luck at the National Spelling Bee. But, as I said before, faith is easy when everything works out so well—like it seems to in your life." He shook his head and began counting the money in his cash register.

"Thank you, sir, for wishing me the best. That is very kind, but I don't know if I will be able to go." Kathleen paused, emotion swelling her throat. "That's what I was trying to tell you. My papa lost his job after the stock market crashed, and we had to move to my grandparents' farm near Archbold, Ohio. Papa has an interview tomorrow, and if he gets the job, then we might have the money for me to travel—otherwise, I'll have to trust that God has something better in store. In His Word it says that God works everything out for good for those who love Him and are called according to His purposes."

Kathleen took off her coat and scarf and unpacked their lunch. She searched for just the right words to say next; she'd learned so much in the past few weeks

about God's plans and how He worked in her life, but she still was pretty new at sharing it with others. "There *are* times when I can't bear the thought of not being able to go to Washington."

The man stopped counting and looked at her intently.

She continued slowly, "I have dreamed so long of being able to go, and I have worked hard on my spelling. However, I am learning to trust that God does what is best, even if I don't understand His overall plan. We never know what God has in store for the next chapter of our lives, and it may be years until we understand. Or, as it is in most story books, we may not understand the grand plot until the end of the book—that is, until we get to Heaven." Kathleen paused a moment, reflecting on what Papa had said that day when she had accidentally shot Old Bruiser, the neighbor's guard dog, then she continued with confidence. "But God, as the author and finisher of our faith, knows the final chapter." Kathleen was surprised at the enthusiasm and courage she felt as she spoke. It amazed her, not only how clearly she remembered Papa's words, but how genuinely she believed them to be true.

"Bold words, little lady, bold words—just you wait. You'll know what I'm talking about when life gets really tough." The shopkeeper shook his head, shoved his money back in his register, and closed it.

The door squeaked open and Papa entered the store. Kathleen shivered when she saw the white steam coming from Papa's heavy breathing. Kathleen could hear gusts of wind whistle down the stovepipe. The temperature must be dropping. She thought of the blizzard they had just been through at the farm and hoped the sudden change in weather did not mean another snowstorm.

"Thank you, Papa, for filling up the car—I'm so thankful you braved the cold in order to take good care of us." Kathleen motioned for him to take a seat at the table she had prepared for their lunch.

Papa took off his gloves, stuffed them in his coat pocket, and then removed his overcoat. He warmed his hands for a moment on the warm stove and then patted Kathleen's red hair. "That's what papas are for—to care for their children's needs." Papa turned to the shopkeeper and invited him to join them for lunch. The little man declined, saying something about a book he was reading.

Kathleen hardly heard a word either of the men said. Her father's words stirred Kathleen's heart and her mind raced.

That is like our Heavenly Father; He cares for all our needs too. She remembered moments when Papa gave her things that, at the time, Kathleen could not possibly see how it could be for the best—like last Christmas when he and Mama had given her schoolbooks. Kathleen smiled at the memory and marveled at how much her perspective had changed in just weeks. At the time she thought it the end of the world. Now she understood and she was grateful.

Had I not received schoolbooks for Christmas, I might have gotten behind in my studies while at Stonehaven.

"Well, lass," said Papa, taking a seat next to her. "What's going on in those shining green eyes of yours? You look so serious—and normally you would have already asked me one hundred questions about Lucy's health."

"I was just thinking that your care for me is a picture of my Heavenly Father's care for us . . . and for Lucy. Now tell me all about Lucy." Kathleen eagerly squeezed her papa's hand. Despite what the little man had said to try to discourage her, her faith felt stronger than ever.

"You are right, lass. Our Heavenly Father is our ultimate provider. No matter how hard I work and pray for the grace and strength to follow in His footsteps, I'll never come close to His perfection. God is the picture of what I strive for. No doubt there will be times in this life when I fail you or let you down, but He will never leave nor forsake you," Papa said, patting the back of her hand. "Should we pray for our food so I can tell you about Lucy?"

"May I pray?" Kathleen asked.

"Of course!" Papa answered emphatically, pride in his eyes.

"Dear Heavenly Father," Kathleen began. "Thank You that You care for us and know us individually, that You have adopted us to be Your children and we can call You 'Father.' My heart is overwhelmed by Your mercy and goodness to Lucy. Thank You for sparing her life. Please continue to heal her body, Lord. We thank You for this food which You have provided and the safety on our journey thus far. Please bless Papa and his job interview tomorrow. We bless Your holy name. Amen."

Kathleen opened her eyes. The little shopkeeper appeared to be listening, but as soon as their eyes met, he quickly looked down at the book he was reading. Kathleen smiled and continued her prayer to herself.

Dear Lord, please soften that gentleman's heart and bring him to a saving knowledge of You.

Kathleen turned to her father. "So, tell me about Lucy. Is she completely out of danger?"

"Dr. Schmitt believes the worst is behind her. Though she is still very weak, she has been on the mend for several days now." Papa took a bite of his ham and cheese sandwich.

There was something he wasn't telling her. "She will be fine now . . . won't she?" Kathleen asked eagerly.

"That is the hope. However, Dr. Schmitt is afraid that the pneumonia has done significant damage to her lungs. He feels that any slight relapse or

new sickness might prove to be grave—that is, until Lucy's lungs have had sufficient time to heal."

"Oh dear! Does that mean she has to be in seclusion?" Had she misheard what Papa had said earlier? Maybe she wouldn't be able to see Lucy after all. All of a sudden her sandwich tasted like cardboard.

"Well, one would think that Dr. Schmitt would quarantine her, but Mr. Meier has asked you to visit as soon as possible—tonight if we arrive early enough. He believes that being around the people she loves most helps to strengthen Lucy. In fact, it wasn't until Peter's visit that Lucy's health began to improve."

"Yes—Lucy loves Peter so much and has missed him miserably. Is Peter still there with her?" Kathleen asked.

"No. He left this very morning. That is why Mr. Meier was so eager to have you come tonight. He said Lucy was bearing Peter's leaving well enough on the outside, but he feared she was hiding her sorrow. He was hoping you could cheer her up."

"Poor Lucy!" Kathleen started to pick up their lunch things. "We had better get going. There is no time to lose! We can eat while we drive, can't we?"

"Whoa there, lass!" Papa put his hand on her arm. "I'm glad to see that you are eager to help your friend, but sit awhile and consider." Papa took her hand and pressed it between his palms. "We are almost finished with our lunch and considering that we are driving in a brand-new Chevrolet sedan with pure white leather seats, I think it best we eat first and then drive." He released his hold and picked up his sandwich. "Besides, lass, it should only delay us ten more minutes at the most." He took a big bite. "Isn't this homemade bread that your Grandma Maggie makes the best thing you ever ate?"

Kathleen settled back in her seat. "Okay, Papa. I see your point." Kathleen thought back to six months before when their car was brand-new. At the time, Papa's company was doing well and he had no way of knowing that the stock market crash would so drastically change their lives. Kathleen saw now, more than ever, the importance of being a wise steward of everything God had placed in their lives.

Papa was right, it did not take long to finish lunch, and she found her appetite had returned. The ham was sliced fresh from a larger piece that had been smoked right on Stonehaven Farm. It was moist and flavorful. For dessert they had Grandma Maggie's sugar cookies that had been baked in her wood stove, old Mary Washington. Kathleen didn't know the secret, but for some reason, they too tasted better than any she'd had before.

Soon Kathleen bundled back up in her coat and scarf. Papa thanked the shopkeeper. After bidding her father good-bye, the man looked at Kathleen.

"My name is Willaby Wallace, and you and your father are welcome here anytime. I enjoyed talking with you, miss. Even though we disagree on some of the most fundamental issues in life, I think you're a real smart girl. Good luck on your spelling bee." The red-headed man bowed deeply as Kathleen walked by.

Kathleen smiled from under the large hood of her red coat, which she had pulled up over her black scarf. "Thank you kindly, Sir Willaby." Kathleen curtsied.

He lifted an eyebrow. It was clear that no one had ever called him that before and it pleased him.

"It was a pleasure meeting you," Kathleen added, "and may God bless you with much faith." She followed Papa out the door into the white world beyond.

Small snowflakes fluttered down and landed on Kathleen's eyelashes. She held out her palms toward the sky. She recalled the long, hard blizzard they had just experienced at the farm. They had been trapped inside for days, but it had seemed more like weeks. "Does it look like a bad storm? Do you think it will slow us down much?" Kathleen looked at her papa's brow. It was furrowed with deep concern.

He stared blankly at the gas pump, rubbed his eyes as if in disbelief, and then scratched his head. "Kathleen, is it my imagination or has our car disappeared?"

Kathleen looked around at where they'd left their car and realized the only reason she was able to see the gasoline pump was because their car, which had been sitting next to it, was gone. She felt her mouth sag open, and for a brief moment her heart froze. "Papa, where's our car?"

CHAPTER

4

An Unwelcome Delay

And we know that in all things God works for the good of those who love him, who have been called according to his purpose.

ROMANS 8:28

Papa bolted out onto the highway, looking up and down the road for their missing car. He called over his shoulder, "I'm going to look for it. Kathleen, you run back inside and call the police. Report a stolen car."

Kathleen felt numb as she turned and raced back up the porch steps of Mr. Wallace's store. Her heart beat in her ears, but no matter how fast she tried to run, it seemed like her legs moved in slow motion. Kathleen felt like she was having a bad dream, but she knew this was real. Their car was gone—stolen. Would they ever see it again?

Kathleen burst through the door, darted around the cashier counter, and grabbed at the phone. In her rush, Kathleen forgot all about asking permission. In fact, she completely forgot all about Mr. Wallace until she heard his squeaky voice directly beneath her.

"Watch out!" he said. "Ouch!" Mr. Wallace was on his hands and knees on the floor getting something from underneath the counter.

"Oh! Excuse me," Kathleen cried as she tripped over his foot. She tried to regain her balance.

Startled by her abrupt intrusion, he sprang up and caught himself in a tangle of Kathleen's long wool coat. Kathleen toppled forward and landed in a disheveled heap on the floor, knocking Mr. Wallace flat. As he sat up, his face was as red as his blazing hair.

"Mr. Wallace! I'm sorry. It's an emergency. I must call the police. Our car is missing!"

"Missing? You mean stolen?" Mr. Wallace jumped to his feet. He was about four inches shorter than Kathleen.

"Yes, I'm afraid it must be." Kathleen picked up the phone receiver and asked the operator to connect her to the police department.

"Those dirty rascals—whoever it was that stole a car from my gas station will pay the penalty," Mr. Wallace shouted as he dashed out the door.

Kathleen hoped that her papa and Mr. Wallace would find signs of the robber by the time she finished reporting the incident to the police. When

Kathleen returned outside, she found both men helplessly searching up and down the street. Reality slowly began to sink in. If their car was not recovered, there would be no way to get to Fort Wayne that afternoon. That meant she wouldn't be able to see Lucy that evening. And if they didn't recover their car soon, Papa might even miss his job interview the next day. Without a car, they could not make the last fifty-five miles of their journey—that is, unless they had enough money for a taxi, bus, or train ride. But even if they did have that money, Kathleen was sure they would need to use it to get back to Stonehaven, not to Fort Wayne. Kathleen bowed her head and closed her eyes.

Dear Heavenly Father, please help us find our car. Lucy needs me. I don't understand why this is happening, but I want to trust You. Please give me Your peace and joy in spite of our circumstances.

The local police arrived in a few minutes. The police chief herded everyone inside the store. He was a tall, burly man with a deep voice that commanded respect. "We'll see what we can do, sir," said the police chief as he wrote down the information. "This county has only had two stolen cars since I've been here, and I was born in Fairview. No one around these parts would do such a thing. Most likely it's a skilled robber from some big city somewhere." The police chief shook his head. "It's a shame to happen to nice folk like you. We'll do everything we can. I'll give you a lift to the police station—unless you'd prefer to wait here."

"You're more than welcome to stay here." Mr. Wallace waved his hand toward the table and stove in the corner. "Food and drinks are on the house."

"Thank you, Willaby. That's very generous of you." Papa turned to the officer. "I think my daughter and I will wait here if you don't mind. Thank you, sir, for all your help." Papa shook hands with the officer.

The next several hours seemed like days as they waited for word of the stolen car. The winds picked up, shook Mr. Wallace's shop, and whistled eerily through the cracks in the walls. The snow was now falling heavily and lined the windowpanes.

Kathleen stood at the window and watched for any sign of their car or of the police returning with good news. "Papa, do you think that the snowstorm will slow the car thief—maybe even stop him in his tracks?"

"It could," Papa said as he added more wood to the stove. He and Mr. Wallace were playing a game of chess.

Mr. Wallace had tried to make them more comfortable. He had brewed a fresh pot of coffee for Mr. McKenzie and offered Kathleen a root beer soda and

a stick of lemon candy. To help the time pass, he had pulled out a chess board, and Papa and Kathleen played several games. Now Kathleen watched as Papa and Mr. Wallace took a turn. Mr. Wallace appeared to be far more concerned and upset about the stolen car than both Papa and Kathleen put together. He had paced the floor and now that he was sitting, he fiddled with one of Papa's pawns that he had captured.

"What's your secret, Mr. McKenzie?" asked Mr. Wallace. He stopped fingering the chess piece and held Papa's gaze. Kathleen could tell he was looking for something more than a trite answer.

Papa's face was sober, but peaceful. "The way I look at it, all we have belongs to the Lord. He knows where that car is, and if we never see it again, He will provide for our needs in another way. I'm just here to steward what He's given me."

Willaby scratched his head. "That's a nice way to look at it, but what about your job interview?" He looked from Papa to Kathleen. "What about the National Spelling Bee?"

Papa glanced at Kathleen. She knew what he was thinking. "It's okay—really, Papa," Kathleen said reassuringly. "I am peaceful with whatever God directs. I know I've had my heart set on it, but . . . it's kind of funny and hard to describe . . . deep in my heart, I am confident I *will* be going to Washington, D.C.—someday. Like you said to me once before, if

this isn't God's timing, He must have something bigger in store. I'm certain He's placed this strong desire in my heart for a special purpose. Perhaps it is a reason that's even greater than winning the nationals."

Mr. Wallace shook his head. "I wish I had your faith." He muttered something more, but Kathleen could not understand. Then straightening his shoulders, he continued, "Mr. McKenzie, please use my phone for any calls you need to make—it's on me. And Kathleen, why don't you call your friend, Lucy. I'm sure it could only encourage her to talk to such a courageous little lady."

"Oh! Thank you, Mr. Wallace." Kathleen clapped her hands together and jumped to her feet. "May I call right now?"

"Make yourself at home." Mr. Wallace bowed his head and waved his hand in the direction of the phone. Kathleen was about to pick up the receiver when the telephone rang.

Startled, Kathleen jumped. "Should I answer it?"

"Yes, yes. Go ahead," Mr. Wallace said.

Kathleen picked up the receiver. "Wallace Gas and General." She'd heard Mr. Wallace answer the phone with those words several times that day. "May I help you? . . . Yes, sir, Mr. McKenzie will be right with you." Kathleen covered the receiver with her hand. "Papa, it's a police officer by the name of O'Henry."

Papa leaped to his feet, and with a few quick strides, he was at the phone. "Hello—yes, this is James McKenzie." Kathleen held her breath, praying that it was good news. "Yes, sir, that is a proper description of my car. Yes, that is my license plate number."

"Do you suppose the officer is just confirming what your pop's car looks like?" Mr. Wallace whispered. He had made his way over to the phone and was standing by Kathleen.

"Astounding!" Papa shook his head in amazement.

"Maybe they've found the car." Kathleen studied Papa's facial expressions, wishing he would say something more definite. "Perhaps the police are in a big chase this very moment," Kathleen whispered.

"Yes, Officer O'Henry, I understand. We'll talk to you in the morning to get an update. Good-bye," Papa said turning to hang the phone up. There was a moment of silence. Papa hung up the phone. When she could see his face she noticed his eyes were twinkling. He knelt. "Come here, lass." Papa opened his arms wide. His grin gave everything away.

"God answered our prayer, didn't He?" Kathleen gave Papa a big hug.

"He did, lass." Papa planted a kiss on Kathleen's forehead. "They found the car abandoned in a ditch near Marysville—about thirty miles from here. The snowstorm is pretty severe down that way, and the

officer thinks the robber must have driven off the road, got stuck in the ditch, and then abandoned the car for fear of getting caught."

"That is amazing, if I do say so myself." Mr. Wallace scratched his head. "Your God sure does seem to be watching out for you."

Kathleen looked at the clock on the wall above the cash register. "It's only five o'clock. Do you think we will still be able to see Lucy this evening?"

"Unfortunately, we won't be able to go anywhere this evening—not in this storm."

Kathleen looked to the floor, trying not to show her disappointment. She was beginning to dislike snow.

"If the weather clears, Officer O'Henry down in Marysville says they hope to get the car out of the ditch with a tow truck first thing in the morning." Papa glanced over at Mr. Wallace. "Is there an inexpensive motel in town where we might stay the night?"

"Mrs. Smith's boardinghouse is about a mile up the road. If she has any spare rooms, I know she would take you in for a night." Mr. Wallace climbed up on his chair and reached for the phone. "I'll call her this very moment. I'm sure if I speak with her, I can get you a very good rate."

CHAPTER

5

On the Road Again

The LORD is good to those whose hope is in him, to the one who seeks him; it is good to wait quietly for the salvation of the LORD.

LAMENTATIONS 3:25–26

Kathleen rubbed her hand affectionately down the smooth white leather seats of their Chevrolet sedan. "Papa, I have never really thought about being grateful for our car, but now that I know what it's like to be without one, it makes me so thankful."

"That it does, lass. That it does." Papa nodded and waved to a passerby as he drove down the highway.

It was a little past noon before their car had been returned by the Marysville police and they were once again on their way to Fort Wayne. Papa had phoned the insurance company to let them know he would not be able to make his morning interview. When he explained their circumstances, the company had been kind enough to reschedule it for later in the afternoon.

Kathleen was so grateful for God's provision. Soon she would see Lucy. The sun was high in the sky and had melted all the snow off the roads. Kathleen's heart was as merry as a bird in spring. She looked forward to telling Lucy all about their adventurous journey with all its odd and exciting twists and turns.

Kathleen's thoughts turned to Mr. Willaby Wallace. Even if she tried to describe the unique man, it would not do him justice. He seemed so tough-hearted and bold at first, but then as they spent more time with him, it was obvious his strong opinions and actions were merely a cover-up for all the hurts and insecurities he held in his heart. By the time they had left, the moat of unbelief in God that surrounded his heart had begun to dry up.

"Thank you for brightening my day—really, my whole life—by your visit today," Mr. Wallace had said as they were leaving. "Your daughter there is a right smart girl. Her faith in God is contagious, and she gave me lots to think about—things I haven't thought about since I was a young boy. And then what you said about God giving you everything . . . and trusting Him to provide all your needs . . . you folks are true Christians—not just 'fair weather' Christians like so many seem to be."

Kathleen was not sure exactly what he meant, but she thought she saw a tear or two in his eyes as he spoke. God had definitely answered her prayers. Once again, circumstances had not turned out the way she expected, but God had been faithful.

They arrived in Fort Wayne with just enough time for Papa to drop Kathleen off at the Meiers' home and make it to his job interview.

"I hope your meeting goes well, Papa. If it does, that means that we can move home," Kathleen said as she stepped out of the car and looked at the familiar surroundings of their neighborhood. Papa was holding the door open for her.

"Thank you, my bonnie lass," Papa said. He shut the passenger door and walked around to the driver's side. "I hope it goes well too. You're not the only one that misses home. I'll see you in a couple of hours."

Kathleen watched the car disappear around the corner and waved good-bye from the Meiers' front door.

Dear God, let my papa's interview go well. If it's Your will, let the insurance company offer him this job so we can return to Fort Wayne. I miss it so much.

She turned and was about to knock when the door opened.

"Kathleeen, you are finally here." Mrs. Meier gave Kathleen a big hug. "I am so thankful you have come.

Lucy has been so sad since her brother left." Kathleen had forgotten that Mrs. Meier had such a thick German accent. She escorted Kathleen inside and up the stairs. "When your papa phoned and told us you were coming, it brightened Lucy's day. You'll have to do most of the talking—she is still very weak, the poor girl." Mrs. Meier put her hand over her heart and slowly shook her head. "Your visit will do her good. Here we are." She quietly opened Lucy's bedroom door and peeked inside. "Very good, you are awake—your friend has made it at last!"

Mrs. Meier opened the door wide and stood aside for Kathleen to enter.

Kathleen's pulse raced as she stepped into the room. Lucy sat propped up with pillows in her bed; her shoulder-length blonde hair draped around her face. All the color was drained from her usually rosy cheeks and cherry red lips. Despite it all, she wore a broad smile that filled the thinned features of her face and brought a twinkle to her blue eyes.

"It really is you!" Lucy reached out her hand.

"Lucy! It's really me." Kathleen rushed forward and took her friend's hand in hers and sat on the bed next to her. She blinked back more than a few tears of joy.

"I never thought I'd get here. I'm so grateful to God that I finally made it."

"Me too," Lucy said, gently squeezing Kathleen's hand. "Since I've been confined to bed, I've thought

about you even more and daydreamed about the adventures you must be having in Ohio. I want to hear every detail of what's happened since I last saw you."

"You won't believe what all has happened at the farm. I actually wrote you pages and pages of letters, but I never got to town to mail them." Kathleen's words tumbled out. "Papa went to town a couple of days ago when I was out with my cousins returning the neighbor's dog that I accidentally shot after rescuing our other neighbors who were buried in their house by the blizzard—well anyway, that's when I got Freddie's letter saying you were sick." Kathleen took Lucy's other hand and paused to take a breath. "Oh, Lucy, I was so dreadfully worried. It was the worst feeling I have ever had—not knowing how sick you were. Papa and I left the very next day to come here. All that to say, I purposed to bring the letters I wrote you, but I was so concerned for your life, I totally forgot."

Lucy shook her head slowly, a knowing smile across her face. "You haven't changed one bit, Kathleen. I'm glad you forgot them; now you can tell me all about what you've been up to in person, and then I can look forward to reading about it later." Lucy turned her head and coughed. It was weak and congested.

"Lucy, have I talked too much? I don't want to tire you out," Kathleen said, standing up.

"Nonsense!" Lucy patted the bed. "Sit back down. I feel stronger now than ever."

But she didn't look strong, and it worried Kathleen that she wasn't as well as everyone had said.

"Now tell me, what is this about shooting a dog? And did I hear you say that you rescued a family whose house was buried in the snow?"

Kathleen sat back on the bed and began to relax as she told Lucy all about her hunting adventure with her older cousin, Bruce, and how she had thought that Mr. Johnston's watchdog was a fearsome wolf stalking her.

"Thankfully, I only wounded him, and we were able to nurse him back to health, but I felt awful about my mistake," Kathleen said.

Lucy was leaning forward, listening wide-eyed to her friend's story, shaking her head in disbelief. "Something like this would only happen to you, Kathleen."

Kathleen noticed a little more color in Lucy's face. Maybe her visit was doing her some good.

"Tell me about the family you rescued."

"The Williamses? They're a family who just moved to Ohio from Alabama. They have six children—three girls and three boys. The oldest is Sharly; she's our age. Anyway, a huge blizzard swept in. It actually snowed for two days straight, and when it was over, there were drifts at least sixteen feet high." Kathleen waved her hand up toward the

ceiling. "Thankfully, our family was well prepared, but the Williamses were caught by surprise." Kathleen went on to describe how she and her cousins, Lindsay, Bruce, and Alex, checked up on them. They found their house buried up to the roof, and they dug them out and brought them food, blankets, and wood for their stove. "They seemed like such a nice family. I can't wait to get to know them better."

"What an amazing story!" Lucy said, clapping her hands together. "It sounds like it came straight out of an adventure novel—Kathleen McKenzie, a true heroine!"

"I wouldn't go that far!" Kathleen laughed, a bit embarrassed at the idea that Lucy thought she had done more than she had. "Bruce and Alex were the real heroes. They knew exactly what to do. Especially Bruce; the way he treated that baby was so tender and kindhearted." Kathleen shook her head. "I would have never guessed. He used to be a cruel prankster when we last visited them—he even locked me in the outhouse once. But that was almost eight years ago. He's changed a lot since then. Now I'm proud to call him my cousin." Kathleen went on to tell Lucy about the drive to Fort Wayne, how their car was stolen, and that she was able to witness to Mr. Willaby Wallace.

Before long Mrs. Meier stepped in the door carrying a tray with ginger cookies and two glasses of milk.

"Kathleen, your papa phoned. He has finished his job interview and is on his way to pick you up. You have just enough time for a little snack."

"So soon?" Lucy frowned.

"You two have been talking for over an hour." Mrs. Meier smiled as she set the tray down on the nightstand. Kathleen could tell she was pleased that Kathleen had come.

"Kathleen, please talk Lucy into trying my cookies—she eats like a bird these days. Hardly touches her food." Kathleen sensed worry behind the teasing tone of Mrs. Meier's voice. She should have noticed sooner just how thin Lucy had become.

"Thank you, Mrs. Meier. I will." Kathleen picked up a cookie and handed it directly to Lucy.

"So your papa had a job interview? Does that mean you might be able to move home soon?" Lucy asked. She eagerly took a bite of the ginger snap.

"Yes! That is—if he gets the job." A knot grew in the middle of Kathleen's stomach. She hoped that her papa was bringing good news, but he'd had so many disappointments over the past several months, she was afraid to hope. Kathleen took a bite of cookie but found it hard to swallow.

"That would be wonderful! Then you and I could be together again, and I can help you study for the National Spelling Bee!" Lucy squeezed Kathleen's hand. "It will be just like old times."

Kathleen took a drink of milk. "That would be wonderful!" Did she dare hope? "I can't wait to hear how his interview went." Kathleen fingered the lace on Lucy's pillowcase. "I am trying not to get my hopes up too high. All we can do is pray for the best." She handed Lucy another cookie and her glass of milk. "The most important thing now is that you get better, and you can't do that without eating."

Papa arrived far too soon and the girls sadly bid each other farewell.

"I'll be praying for you every day." Kathleen bent down and gave Lucy a long hug. "I miss you already."

Kathleen could not wait to find out about Papa's interview.

"So—did you get the job, Papa?" she asked as soon as they drove away from the Meiers' house.

Papa reached over and affectionately squeezed Kathleen's shoulder. She could sense by the look in his eye what his answer was going to be. "I'm afraid not, lass—not yet, anyway. They had already filled the spot by the time I arrived this afternoon. They said had I been there earlier this morning, I would have gotten it." Kathleen could read disappointment on his face, but then he brightened. "They did say I had an impressive résumé, and they would keep it on file for the future." Papa turned and gave her an encouraging smile.

"I'm sorry, Papa." Kathleen looked out the window, trying to hold back tears of disappointment. Being back in Fort Wayne made her miss her own home even more. She longed to go back to Hogeland Junior High and be with the friends and teachers that she was used to. But most of all, she wanted so much to be back home so she could be with Lucy. Kathleen also knew that going to the National Spelling Bee was now no longer a possibility. There was one thing she had learned in the past months: God had a bigger and better plan than her dreams.

Dear God, help me to be strong and trust You fully. I want to walk in Your ways and be thankful in all things—please give me the grace to be thankful right now, even though I don't understand. Thank You, Jesus. Amen.

CHAPTER

6

Springtime

See! The winter is past; the rains are over and gone. Flowers appear on the earth; the season of singing has come.

SONG OF SONGS 2:11–12

Kathleen looked up from the letter she was reading from Lucy and breathed deeply of the fresh spring air that drifted through Lindsay's open bedroom window. She whispered a prayer of gratefulness. Lucy was doing well and gaining strength. Time had marched forward as it always does. Signs of spring were appearing each day, and Kathleen was as happy as the robin that sang outside Lindsay's bedroom window each morning. She loved spring. Stonehaven had become her home away from home.

Standing, Kathleen leaned out the window to soak in the noonday sunshine. "Look, Lindsay! The apple tree outside your window has tiny buds on it!"

Lindsay, who was sitting on the bed and finishing up her homework assignment for the weekend, jumped up to join her at the window. She put her arm around Kathleen's shoulder and smiled. "Soon it will be so warm in this room we won't have to put heating stones in bed with us and we can leave the windows open all night long," Lindsay laughed. "I'll never forget how cold you looked that first week here at Stonehaven. I was sure you wouldn't last a week here on the farm, but I was wrong."

Kathleen's thoughts went back to when her family first moved to the farm. It now seemed so long ago. She remembered how naïve she'd been at first about living on the farm and going without electricity and indoor plumbing. In fact, when she noticed the patches on her cousins' clothing and saw that Lindsay's nightgown and undergarments were made from flour sacks, she feared that they might all starve that winter. How wrong she had been. Even though Uncle John said the crops had not been good that year and the wheat and corn prices were down, Kathleen had never gone hungry. In fact, their meals were far more bountiful on the farm than they were in the city, and Lindsay said with the fresh fruit and vegetables from the garden, they ate even better during the summer months.

Kathleen's relationship with her cousins had grown too, especially her friendship with Lindsay, whose shyness seemed to melt away with the snow. In fact, Kathleen was often caught off guard with just how talkative Lindsay could be.

"Guess what next week is?" Lindsay said, interrupting Kathleen's thoughts.

"The first week of spring?"

"No, spring is already here. Next week is Easter Sunday. You know what that means, don't you?" Lindsay threw herself back on the bed.

Kathleen wondered what she was talking about. "It means our mothers are going to sing a duet at church and we are going to accompany them—me with my harmonica and you with your mandolin. But why are you so excited? I thought you didn't like performing in front of people."

"Oh! Please, don't remind me," Lindsay groaned. "That's not what I'm talking about! I was thinking about something far more pleasant. Easter Sunday means you and I will get new dresses."

A shadow passed over Kathleen's heart. Her father had now been out of a job for almost six months, and she knew that there would be no money for a new dress. She sighed at the thought of her papa. He had been in Fort Wayne looking for work more often than he was at Stonehaven the past couple of months. He would be leaving again right after Easter. She missed him miserably each time he had to go.

Kathleen remembered her beautiful lavender silk dress she had worn last year on Easter Sunday. She

had tried it on last week, hoping it would still fit in spite of her growth spurt, but it was several inches above her knees. Each time Papa came back from Fort Wayne, he would exclaim, "Kathleen, if you don't stop growing, I'll have to put bricks on your head. Where has my little girl gone anyway?" She sighed. Maybe her Grandma Maggie had some scrap material Mama could add to the bottom of last year's dress.

"Kathleen, are you okay?" Lindsay asked.

"Oh . . . yes! I—I'm glad you get a new dress, Lindsay, but I think I'll wear last year's Easter dress."

"Whatever for? You've grown two or three inches since then. Don't you think it will be too short? Besides, I was looking forward to you and I picking out the feed sacks together when we go to town today. They have such pretty patterns these days at Smith's Feed and Seed. I know it might sound odd to you, but it really is fun digging through the bags of feed for just the right design to make into a dress. Although, I don't know if I'll ever find a print that I like more than the one I found last spring."

Lindsay pulled a bright red dress with cheery white daisies out of the trunk at the foot of her bed. Kathleen caught her breath—it truly was a stylish dress.

"Do you mean to tell me you made that from—from a feed sack?"

"Of course, silly. Didn't you know that almost all of my dresses are made from gunny, flour, or chicken feed sacks?" Lindsay held the dress up next to her. It clearly was too short, but Kathleen could tell that the color of the dress was perfect with Lindsay's blonde hair.

There wasn't a day that went by without Kathleen being astonished at one thing or another about farm life.

"Your dress is beautiful. I would have never guessed it came from a feed sack. But—"

"But what? Kathleen McKenzie, are you too embarrassed to stand up in church wearing something someone else might have seen at Mr. Smith's?" Lindsay twirled around the room with her old Easter dress. "If so, I wouldn't worry too much about it. Almost everyone around here gets their material from the same supplier."

"It's not that. It's just that Papa still doesn't have a job, and I don't think we can even afford a feed sack." Tears burned Kathleen's eyes and threatened to spill over. She sat on Lindsay's bed staring intently at the Dresden Plate quilt Grandma Maggie had made.

Lindsay laid her dress on her nightstand and sat down next to Kathleen. She put her arm around her shoulder. "Kathleen, don't you know? Pa buys lots of feed bags each year and there will be plenty of material to go around. Our mothers and Grandma will be able to have new aprons, and if we find the right print,

the little boys will even have a dress shirt for their Sunday best."

"Really? Are—are you sure I wouldn't be imposing?" Kathleen gently ran her fingers down Lindsay's Easter dress and imagined how nice it would be to have a new outfit.

"Of course it's fine. We have to buy the feed for the livestock anyway—Pa wouldn't be spending more than he normally does."

"In that case, I can't wait to wear a feed sack dress." Kathleen put her arm around Lindsay. "Thanks."

Kathleen hurried to finish her letter to Lucy before their midday meal. That way she could take it with her when they drove into town and mail it from the post office that very afternoon.

During lunch, Uncle John informed them he would need Papa, Grandpa, Alex, and Bruce at the farm that afternoon. "Lindsay, you'll have to drive the horse and wagon to town by yourself, lass." As he talked, he sliced off a thick piece of ham that the women had baked for lunch. It was one that had been smoked right on the farm.

"Lindsay has never driven that far before," said Aunt Elizabeth, looking at Uncle John with a bit of worry on her face. She set a bowl of mashed potatoes on the table.

"I have all the confidence in the world that the girls will manage just fine." Grandpa pointed at the little boys who were sitting at one end of the table, wiggling with excitement. "I've told Robby and Richard that you and Kathleen are in charge today, so see to it that they mind their manners. I'll have Alex hitch up the team after breakfast while I write a list of supplies for the feed and seed store."

Kathleen looked from Uncle John to her papa with a questioning look. Uncle John acted as though it was perfectly normal to send a twelve-and a thirteen-year-old girl into town on errands, but Kathleen was not sure what her papa would say.

He just smiled knowingly and nodded his head. "Your uncle and I used to drive the wagon to town all the time when we were your age. We have all sorts of exciting memories . . . like the time the horses spooked." Papa laughed and looked toward his brother. "They ran at least a mile before your Uncle John and I were able to settle them. We never did figure out what scared the horses that day . . ."

"James, are you sure it's safe?" asked Kathleen's mother. "Kathleen doesn't know the first thing about driving a team of horses."

"Don't worry, Claire. The girls will manage just fine." Papa affectionately ran his finger down Kathleen's nose.

Richard abruptly placed his glass of milk on the table. "Do you think that these horses might spook today?" He looked up at Bruce with a broad milk mustache and wide eyes.

"Sure, it's safe." Bruce tousled Richard's blond hair. "The horses they had back then weren't as gentle as Daisy and Dan, and besides, Lindsay handles the horses as well as Alex. It will be fine. I promise."

"Whoa! Wait a minute; I'm not so sure I agree with that," Alex said as he helped himself to another generous serving of mashed potatoes. "Granted, Lindsay is good, but if the team were to spook and run away with her, they'd be halfway to Fort Wayne before Lindsay had the strength to rein them in."

"Tush, Tush! That will be enough talk about runaway horses." Grandma Maggie waved her hand as if she were shooing away a bothersome fly. "Lindsay and Kathleen are right smart lassies. They will handle the team just fine. Besides, Dan and Daisy are as gentle as wee little lambs—they haven't spooked since they were fillies frolicking in the fields."

Kathleen looked up at Mama, who was sitting quietly with her hands folded. She hadn't seemed happy about the situation. Now, after Bruce's comment, Mama seemed even more unsettled, but she didn't say another word. Kathleen was sure it was because she was outvoted. For the first time she wondered how it must be for her mama to adjust to

life on the farm. Everything—even their family life—was so different than it had been back in Fort Wayne. Maybe Kathleen wasn't the only one who had to make adjustments.

Before they left the farm, Mama and Aunt Elizabeth had all sorts of advice for the girls concerning what prints would look best with certain dress styles. "I've told the boys that they can pick their own feed bag for their shirts," Aunt Elizabeth whispered to the girls as they eagerly bounded up into the wagon seat. "Just watch Robby. Make sure his isn't too wild." Richard and Robby climbed into the back of the wagon, pushing and shoving each other playfully as they did. They reminded Kathleen of a couple of puppies she'd seen once at the park in Fort Wayne. She wasn't sure that Robby was the only wild one they needed to watch on this trip.

Kathleen noticed her mother's face looked a little pinched as she waved good-bye. "Do be careful," she called as Lindsay clucked to the horses and they trotted down the lane.

It was a warm day, and the few patches of dirty snow on the side of the roads were quickly melting. The county road was muddy and quite rutted, making the seven miles to town a long, bumpy trip. Though Kathleen enjoyed the novelty of riding in a wagon behind horses, she was not used to the feel of it. Grandpa McKenzie had a Model T, but he rarely used it. Money was scarce and buying gasoline was low on the list of priorities. Papa too chose the horse and buggy over his car—except, of course, when he traveled for job interviews.

By the time they arrived at Smith's Feed and Seed, they were all glad to get out of the wagon and stretch their legs. The front of the store looked like a red and white barn with a large covered front opening. On it were stacked piles of brightly printed feed sacks. Inside the store, there were more piles of feed. Some stacks were over Richard's head, and some were as tall as Lindsay. In the back, near the enormous loading dock doors, were large bales of hay. The walls were covered with all sorts of tin posters—each with a catchy slogan advertising a brand of feed and seed as the best.

Kathleen breathed deeply of the rich smell of seed sacks and hay. The scent reminded her of the barn at Stonehaven, but much more pleasing. Kathleen attributed that mostly to the fact that there were no animal stalls to be cleaned.

After greeting Mr. Smith, Lindsay handed the weathered older gentleman her father's supply list. Then, much to Kathleen's surprise, Mr. Smith let them rummage through the stacks of feed and seed sacks, so they could find just the right prints.

"Let my assistant, William, and me know which bags you want." Mr. Smith waved his hand toward a young man who was sweeping the floor near the loading dock. "You know William Scott, the pastor's son, don't you?"

"Yes, sir." Lindsay's cheeks flushed, and she quickly brushed her hand over her waistline to smooth the wrinkles from her dress. Kathleen had been surprised when Lindsay had changed into it from the pants that she wore every day on the farm. Now she saw the reason why.

"Anyway, he will load them up for you and I'll write a bill for your pa," Mr. Smith said, glancing down at the supply list Uncle John had sent.

Kathleen noticed that the tall, dark-haired William had briefly stopped sweeping to smile and tip his hat to Lindsay. Lindsay's face flushed even redder, as if that were possible. She nodded her head in acknowledgement and rushed behind a stack of large grain sacks.

"Kathleen, look at this blue and white paisley. Isn't that a nice pattern?" Lindsay asked.

Kathleen stifled a laugh. "It's lovely." It was so obvious that Lindsay and the pastor's son were sweet on each other and that Lindsay's sudden interest in a fifty-pound bag of chicken feed was just a cover. Kathleen would have to ask her cousin about William later; right now her focus was on picking out her favorite printed grain sack.

At first, Kathleen could not make up her mind. She ran her fingers over the cotton sacks and tried to imagine how each one would look if it was transformed into a dress. There were all sorts of colors—from bright yellow to pale blue, deep red to light green—and many different prints to choose between. Lindsay was partial to the more muted paisleys with swirls, and Kathleen preferred the more vibrant colors with small flowers dancing across the print.

"We should try to match a little, don't you think? After all, we must consider what we'll look like standing up in front of church together with our instruments," Kathleen suggested.

Lindsay's face turned pale. "Why did you have to remind me?" She leaned against a stack of cattle feed.

"Don't worry, no matter how badly you mess up, you could not possibly be as bad as I was last summer at our mission's conference." Kathleen's face burned at the memory. "I decided to use my brand-new harmonica, which was nothing like my old one, and—well, you can imagine the rest."

After going back and forth for almost an hour, the girls finally came to a decision. The boys had made their choices right away and had given up on the girls long ago. Robby had fallen asleep on top of a pile of soft feed sacks in the back corner of the room, and Richard had found some children and they were at the entrance of the store playing jacks.

"Richard, what do you think of our sacks?" Kathleen asked. "My dress will be the bright blue with pink roses, and Lindsay will make hers from the pink and white paisley. Do you think they blend well?" Kathleen was eager to get an opinion on their choices—even if the opinion was coming from her nine-year-old brother.

Richard looked at the two town boys kneeling on the ground beside him and then up at Kathleen. He shrugged. "They look nice to me. I like the one with the roses especially."

One of the boys snickered and repeated in a girly voice, "I like the one with the roses."

Richard tried to ignore his comment and focused intently on the game of jacks, but Kathleen could see Richard's face turning as red as an apple.

Kathleen immediately felt bad that she had embarrassed him in front of his friends.

"Of course, what would you know about stuff like this? You know we have to be going. Bruce is breaking his foal this afternoon, and he told me he needed your help. He said that you were the only one brave enough to get near it."

The two boys looked at Richard with a little more respect at that comment.

"Good day to you, boys." Kathleen looked them straight in the eyes to let them know that everything would be fine so long as they did not mess with her

little brother. Richard's face lit up at the mention of working with the horses, and he straightened his shoulders and followed Kathleen to the wagon where they were already loading their supplies.

Lindsay seemed relieved to see them. "Richard, tell William which bags you and Robby chose so he can load them up. I don't want to wake Robby until the last possible moment." Lindsay bent down to show Mr. Smith the sacks that she and Kathleen had picked out for their dresses and for their mothers' and Grandma Maggie's new aprons.

CHAPTER

7

Easter Preparations

He has made everything beautiful in its time. He has also set eternity in the hearts of men; yet they cannot fathom what God has done from beginning to end.

ECCLESIASTES 3:11

Stonehaven was a welcome sight by the time Lindsay drove the wagon full of tired but satisfied shoppers into the farmyard. As Kathleen expected, Mama, Aunt Elizabeth, and Grandma all rushed out to greet them, anxious to view their purchases. Even Grandpa put down the harness he was mending on his front porch to join in the event.

"I see you all made it back in one piece." Grandpa patted the draft horse Daisy on the shoulder. "No runaway horses?" He winked at Kathleen. "Daisy and Dan must have behaved themselves today."

"Richard, is this yours? It will make a wonderful dress shirt for you." Mama pointed to a hunter green grain bag with a pattern of flying ducks. She really did not have to ask. Ever since Bruce had promised to take him duck hunting next fall, it was all Richard talked about.

Before Richard could answer, Robby pointed out his choice with a big grin. "Do you like mine, Aunt Claire? It has puppies on it that look just like the one I've always wanted. I picked it out all by myself." Robby proudly patted the feed sack and grinned from ear to ear, failing to notice the shock on everyone's faces. The feed sack that Robby prized so much was a lovely pink with little black dogs wearing bright blue bows around their necks.

"Do you mean to tell me you picked that out—by yourself?" Aunt Elizabeth tried to hide the smile that shined in her eyes and threatened to spill out on her face.

Richard shrugged. "Don't blame me. I tried to tell him."

Lindsay put her hand over her mouth. "Oh, Mama, I forgot to check what he'd picked out. We were in such a hurry."

Aunt Elizabeth looked at her skeptically. "In a hurry? Or was there something or perhaps someone there who was distracting you?"

Lindsay blushed.

"Alex, Bruce, come see the puppies I picked out," called Robby as he skipped toward the barn to find his older brothers. Kathleen watched him go, glad she would not have to be the one to tell him that he would not be wearing little puppies with blue bows on Easter Sunday.

~

Each evening, after finishing their homework assignments, Kathleen and Lindsay carefully cut and sewed their dresses on Aunt Elizabeth's treadle machine. At first Kathleen found the machine awkward, but Grandma Maggie showed her how to rock the pedal with a steady foot and gently guide the fabric with her hand. Slowly, the dresses began to take shape. Kathleen held up the bodice and looked admiringly at the crisp, white collar, puffed sleeves, and thin belt that would trim the waistline. She could not believe how a sack of feed could be made to look so beautiful.

Poor Robby's hopes were dashed when his mother broke the news to him that boys did not wear pink prints that were meant for little girls. Instead, she made him a shirt out of a brown paisley that Mr. Smith had thrown in to fill the order. No matter what anyone said, Robby was convinced that the puppy print was far nicer than the dull brown.

By Saturday evening, the girls had placed the last stitch in the hem, and they were ready to give their dresses the Sunday morning début.

"Let's try on our dresses and see how they look when we stand next to each other," Kathleen suggested. Before Kathleen moved to Stonehaven, Lindsay never thought about her appearance or what anybody might think about whether she matched or not.

Kathleen, on the other hand, had learned from Lindsay that it is not what you're wearing on the outside that matters as much as the condition of your heart. Mother and Aunt Elizabeth would just smile at the two of them and say that they balanced each other wonderfully. Kathleen could learn to care a little less about her appearance and focus more on the heart, and Lindsay could learn the importance of being tidy both in her dress and personal grooming.

The girls rushed to Lindsay's room eager to change. They twirled and spun in front of the tall mirror until they had seen every angle. After one year of the same Sunday dress, Lindsay was thrilled with her new one, and Kathleen was pleased and grateful to have a new dress.

Lindsay blushed with pleasure as Kathleen complimented her dress. "I like the bell sleeves, and the thin cream ribbon trimming on your collar blends well with the pink paisley print. You look so stylish and

quite grown up." Kathleen dramatically waved her hand down the lines of Lindsay's dress. "I'd say you look fourteen instead of just thirteen. If you curled your hair and pinned it up, you would look sixteen. Hmm . . . sixteen, that's courting age, isn't it? Let's see, who might be at church on Sunday that might notice my beautiful cousin . . . ?" Kathleen put her chin in her hand and tapped her fingers on her face. "You know, it's not fair that you look so nice. You might distract a certain someone from the sermon."

Lindsay placed her hand over her mouth in shock. "Kathleen McKenzie, I cannot imagine who you're talking about. Besides, you know my hair is as straight as a board. Even if I pinned it up, it would be undone before we got to church." Lindsay's rosy cheeks deepened to a crimson as she spoke.

"You know who I'm talking about just as much as Pastor Scott's son knows who I'm referring to." Kathleen loved teasing her cousin about William, and she could tell Lindsay didn't mind that much as long as it wasn't in front of her brothers.

"I don't know why you think William is interested in me. I've hardly ever talked to him. Besides, I'm thirteen, not sixteen, and that's certainly not courting age."

"I know you're not sixteen, but that doesn't mean you can't put curls in your hair, pin it up, and look pretty, does it?"

"Look, I know you tie your hair up in rags every night, and they produce handsome curls each morning, but how do you suppose that this could become curly?" Lindsay held up a thick strand of her straight golden hair. "My hair is so long and heavy it will take more than a few rags to bend it."

Kathleen grabbed a handful of Lindsay's hair. "That *is* a problem." It could not have been straighter even if she had pressed it with a hot iron. But Kathleen was determined that they should arrive at church in style. Newly inspired, Kathleen jumped up and ran toward the door. "I have an idea. I'll be right back. You just stay put."

Kathleen had remembered a stack of old-fashioned women's magazines in the attic of her grandma's house. She rushed downstairs, grabbed a lantern, and was off across the yard to Grandma and Grandpa's. No one would wonder where she was going. She needed to say good night to her parents anyway.

Soon she was heading back to her uncle's house with several magazines tucked under her arm. Kathleen smiled to herself. A few months ago, she would have been terrified of wolves if she had to walk alone on the farm at night, but now she barely even thought twice about going anywhere alone at Stonehaven. It seemed that the worst of everything was behind her now.

Kathleen paused briefly on the porch and looked up at the stars. The warmth of spring was just around the corner, and soon all of Stonehaven would be bursting with life and hope. From the barn, she heard the quiet bawl of a newborn calf. How appropriate it was that Resurrection Sunday was always in the spring. It was such a wonderful reminder of new life—not only in the blossoming world around her, but also of the new life in Christ that God gave everyone.

Kathleen took a deep, contented breath and then turned to go inside. She lightly skipped up the stairs, passing Bruce at the top. He stopped abruptly.

"My, my, what have we here?" He grabbed one of the magazines out of her hands. "*Ladies' Home and Etiquette*. May I join in on the reading tonight?"

Kathleen felt a moment of panic. Did he suspect what she was up to? "We would love for you to help us practice our manners." Kathleen waved the lantern in the direction of Lindsay's room and curtsied in mock seriousness. She hoped Bruce did not notice the sudden flush that burned her cheeks.

Bruce laughed. "Too bad I have to check on the cows." He handed her back the magazine. "Several of them are due to calve anytime now. You'll have to give me etiquette lessons some other time." Bruce chuckled.

Kathleen felt relieved that she had gotten by without him asking too many questions. She pushed Lindsay's

door open with her foot and plunked the stack of magazines on the bed. "Here's my idea."

Lindsay brought the lantern near and looked curiously through the pile of periodicals. "*Lady's Bazaar, Godey's Lady's Book, Women's Home Journal* . . . Whatever are these—and—and where in heaven's name did you dig them up? There's more dust and dirt on these old things than there is in Grandma's rose garden." Lindsay slowly flipped through the one titled *Godey's Lady's Book.*

"I found them tucked back in a corner of Grandma Maggie's attic just the other day. This is what our mothers would have read when they were our age—or at least when they were courting age. I asked Grandma Maggie about them, and she said they had everything in them from the latest dress styles, to common courting etiquette, to the best way to wash your bloomers, and even how to groom your hair. Grandma Maggie told me that I could look at them, but I was afraid the boys might tease me. Then I forgot all about them—that is, until now." Kathleen jumped up on the bed next to Lindsay and eagerly flipped through the pages.

"So, tell me again, why is it that we are looking at these? I thought you were going to curl my hair," Lindsay said, looking a bit confused.

"That is what I'm doing. I remember seeing something about a special technique for hair curling in one

of these magazines, but I don't quite remember which . . . wait a minute. I've found it." Kathleen read the directions out loud.

Hair-Curling Liquid for Ladies

Take 2 ounces borax and 1 drab Gum Senegal (in powder); add 1 quart hot water (not boiling). Stir, and as soon as ingredients are dissolved, add 2 ounces spirit of wine strongly impregnated with camphor. On retiring to rest, wet the locks with the above liquid and roll them on twists of paper as usual. Leave them till morning when they may be unwrapped and formed into ringlets.

"The Small Belongings of Dress," 1894

"I'm not so sure we have all those ingredients," said Lindsay, scanning the article.

"We may not have Gum Senegal—or however you say it." Kathleen wrinkled her nose. "But it only calls for a drab. That can't be very much. We have plenty of borax. I used it on the clothes when we were doing wash the other day, and I have seen a bottle of camphor in the medicine cabinet." Kathleen threw the magazine to the side and jumped to her feet.

"Grandpa has a little wine stashed away that he uses for medicinal purposes. Surely he wouldn't mind if we borrowed a bit," Lindsay said. "But I'm still not so sure I want to do this. What if it doesn't work?"

"Let's give it a try. It couldn't hurt anything. I'll put some in my hair too." Kathleen took Lindsay's hand and headed to the door. "Most everyone is in bed by now, so if our experiment doesn't work, then no one will need to know. And if it does, they will all be surprised by our stylish hairdos."

CHAPTER

8

A Dreadful Mistake

Consider it pure joy, my brothers, whenever you face trials of many kinds, because you know that the testing of your faith develops perseverance.

JAMES 1:2–3

After much convincing, Lindsay finally agreed to let Kathleen curl her hair with the magazine's concoction.

"Okay, let's split the list of supplies and meet back here." Lindsay grabbed the lantern that was hanging on a hook near her door. Soon they were quietly scurrying all over the house, gathering the ingredients as quietly as possible. Kathleen smiled as she envisioned the look on William's face when he saw Lindsay's hair all done up. Lindsay was pretty enough without even trying, but given any effort, she would be the prettiest girl in the county—at least the prettiest of all the girls Kathleen had seen. The only problem was Lindsay never cared to try to look pretty.

Kathleen's mother always reminded her that this was not a character flaw. "True beauty comes from your heart," her mama had told Kathleen when they first moved to the farm. "Lindsay is not a sloppy girl by any means—that would be a flaw. Having a pure conscience, joyful spirit, and genuine love for those around you makes all the difference in the world, and that is what really makes Lindsay stand out among the other girls in the county."

That was okay, but Kathleen was glad that she had talked Lindsay into dressing up for Easter Sunday. She knew Lindsay would finally see how important it was to look good on the outside too.

Before long they had boiled water on the stove, had procured the necessary ingredients, and were safely back in their room.

"Has the water in the kettle cooled enough? The directions say that it should not be boiling," Kathleen said, placing four ounces of borax in the mixing bowl.

"I'm pretty sure it's cooled enough. Are we doubling the recipe? Looks like you put a heap of that stuff in the bowl." Lindsay studied the recipe in the magazine and then looked again at the mixture.

"I want to make sure there's plenty of curling liquid for both of us." Kathleen watched as Lindsay

poured what she estimated to be two quarts into the bowl.

"Are you sure that's enough water?" Kathleen asked.

"It looks awfully thick, but I'm almost positive that I put the right amount in this time—I'm always getting ounces, pints, quarts, and gallons mixed up though. And I'd seriously doubt whether or not I have it right this time, except for the fact that Mother just reminded me the other day that there are sixteen ounces in a quart and four quarts in a gallon. That would mean that I need to double the amount of water than there is of the borax. Right?" Kathleen had blocked out Lindsay's confusing logic long before and her thoughts were off to the next step.

"Sounds fine to me. As soon as the borax dissolves, you can pour in the wine and camphor—it says the wine is to be 'strongly impregnated with camphor.' I suppose that means we'll have to use a lot of it." It did not register to Kathleen that her cousin had again mixed up her measurement, pouring only eight ounces of water—half of a quart—into the mixture instead of two whole quarts.

"Phew, this camphor sure smells strong. I'm not so convinced that I want it in my hair," Lindsay said, blinking her eyes against the strong odor.

"Don't worry, Lindsay. We'll just add a little bit of Grandmother's rose water and we'll smell as fresh

as a spring breeze." Kathleen tried to sound confident, but the mixture smelled so foul she wrinkled her nose.

The girls browsed through other recipes in the magazines, substituting and adding all sorts of extra ingredients before they were absolutely confident that they had the perfect mixture to top all others. It did look thicker and smell stronger than Kathleen had imagined, but she was determined to arrive at church the next morning with curls in Lindsay's hair, and she convinced herself that everything would work out perfectly.

Kathleen smeared the pasty mixture on the tips of Lindsay's thick, blonde hair and rolled it up with strips of rags. The directions said to use bits of paper, but that was too precious of a commodity to be sliced into strips and wrapped in their hair. Paper had to be saved for her school studies. The few extra sheets she had at the end of the week she used strictly to write letters to her friends back home—especially Lucy, whom she missed more than anything.

Kathleen shook her head thinking about how much had changed since last Easter. She would never have dreamed that they would be living on a farm without enough money to purchase an Easter dress or even buy a spare sheet of paper. The funny thing about their situation was that even though Madelyn and Patricia Barnett and other folks back in Fort

Wayne would consider them poor, Kathleen did not feel like they were. She didn't even mind wearing a dress made from patched-together feed sacks. In fact, Kathleen was convinced that Lindsay and she would look as lovely as any of her friends back home in Fort Wayne on this Easter Sunday.

"Ouch!" shouted Lindsay. "Do you have to wrap my hair that tightly against my head?"

"I'm sorry; I wasn't paying attention. My thoughts were hundreds of miles away."

"I've never been that far away from here. In fact, I've never traveled farther than town. I don't think I would ever care to, either," Lindsay said in her matter-of-fact way.

"But you're missing so much. Someday I'm going to take you to Fort Wayne and show you what life in the big city is like. There are all sorts of exciting things to do and places to go. We could go to the cinema and watch a moving picture and then after that go to my favorite soda shop and get a scrumptious chocolate malt or a root beer float." Kathleen closed her eyes and licked her lips at the memory.

"We have malts at the druggist in town," Lindsay shrugged. "I don't know why I'd have to travel all the way to Fort Wayne just for that."

"But what about seeing a moving picture; doesn't that sound exciting? I could bring you to Wolf and Dessauer's department store—you can't even begin to

imagine how many wonderful things they have for sale there. Everything from dresses to dolls and from fancy shoes to fine china tea sets." A shadow passed over Kathleen's face. She separated a strand of hair from Lindsay's head and began to wrap it around another rag. "Even if we don't have the money to buy anything, it is still fun to go to the department store just to look."

"Sounds interesting enough, but I'm still just as happy here," Lindsay said.

Kathleen could not fathom her cousin never wanting to explore beyond this farming community. She desperately wanted to convince Lindsay that there was a great big exciting world out there, but it was no use. Kathleen had tried before, and it was like trying to speak to her in a different language. She rolled the last strand of hair on Lindsay's head. Someday, when they were grown, maybe Lindsay would change her mind and they could travel the world together.

"Kathleen, are your fingers tingling?" Lindsay asked as she began to roll Kathleen's hair.

Kathleen looked down at her own fingers. They were red and burned. "They do hurt a little. I wonder why?"

"It's probably from that strong-smelling camphor or one of the other ingredients we threw in there." Lindsay finished rolling Kathleen's hair and then quickly poured

what was left of the warm water in the kettle into the washbasin on her dresser, and both girls sank their hands deep within the soothing waters.

Much to the girls' relief, the burning sensation eased after a thorough soaking. "You don't suppose that stuff is burning our hair like this?" asked Lindsay.

Kathleen thought about curling irons. They would burn her hands, but not her hair. "I think hair is tougher than skin."

"Yeah, I suppose you're right," said Lindsay. "Don't I look funny with my hair all tied up like this?" She whirled around in front of the mirror taking one last look before jumping into bed.

"You don't look any funnier than I do every night before bed." Kathleen looked down at her hands and shook her head. "It's a wonder to me that the directions did not mention anything about it burning your skin." Kathleen shrugged, blew out the lantern, and joined Lindsay who was already snuggled deep within the quilts and bedding.

The girls woke with the first rays of sunlight that peeked through their bedroom window.

Kathleen jumped out of bed. "Lindsay, hurry and get up. Let's go do our chores and get back here as fast as we can. I can't wait to see how your curls look. Our

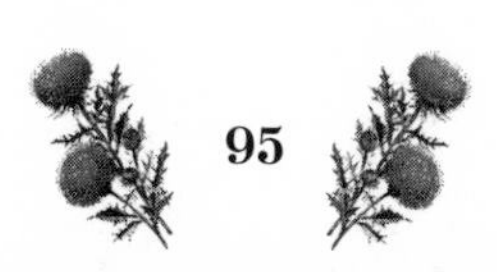

mothers will be so surprised." She pulled her work clothes over her head.

Lindsay touched her hair. "How are we going to keep it a surprise? Won't they notice something is different about me?"

Kathleen looked around the room. "I know. Let's wear our winter caps so they won't know we have our hair tied up."

"That's a great idea." Lindsay quickly dressed and then covered her hair. Her eyes glowed with excitement. It reminded Kathleen of how she felt on Christmas morning.

The plan worked perfectly and before long the cows were milked, the chickens fed, and the eggs gathered without the slightest suspicion as to why the girls had their heads bundled up so warmly. They rushed back to their rooms to change into their new dresses and fix their hair before breakfast.

"I can't wait to see the look on Mother's face." Kathleen giggled as she and Lindsay raced up the stairs and closed the door.

"I wonder what they'll say?" said Lindsay.

"They probably won't even recognize us." Kathleen imagined the pride in her father's eyes as he saw how she'd transformed her cousin from a farm girl into a beauty.

Kathleen ripped off her hat. Her hands trembled in anticipation as she untied the first rag and slowly

unrolled a lock of her red hair. Kathleen and Lindsay both gazed into the full-length mirror, anxious to see the outcome.

Kathleen gasped in complete shock. Instead of a shiny curl bouncing back from the end of the rag, she watched in utter dismay as a brittle, frazzled piece of hair broke from her head and dropped to the floor. "Oh, my goodness! What has happened? What ever are we going to do?"

Lindsay, who was too shocked to speak, just looked with large, unbelieving eyes from the brittle curl on the ground to what was left of the blunt, frazzled ends on Kathleen's head. There were at least five inches of her hair gracing the floor, which left only four on her head. With grave silence, Lindsay soberly stared at her hair.

"Well, I think you—you'll look very cute with your hair in a b-bob," Lindsay finally stammered. She sounded positive, but Kathleen could see Lindsay's eyes welling up in tears. Lindsay always wore her hair long. In fact, Kathleen was pretty sure that, with the exception of a few trims, she had never had it cut.

"Yes, a bob will look nice—nice and youthful." Kathleen sighed in utter anguish. She wanted to cry, but she couldn't—she wouldn't for Lindsay's sake.

"At least we have some hair left—I wonder which ingredient burned our h-hair off?" Lindsay said as she quickly let down her first lock and watched a large clump break and fall to the floor. Her lips quivered and tears threatened to spill from her clear blue eyes as she stared blankly at the growing pile on the ground. Soon there was a heap of frayed, brittle red and blonde hair on the floor. Kathleen and Lindsay looked helplessly at their shocking reflections in the mirror.

"That's what I was afraid of," Lindsay lamented.

"What? Did you think this would happen to us last night?"

"No! If I had any idea things would turn out this way, I wouldn't have let you talk me into it."

"Then whatever were you afraid of?" Kathleen said, much perplexed by the whole situation.

"When I first saw the end of your hair—how it is so frazzled? I was afraid we would end up looking like—like the messed-up straw wig on our old scarecrow."

"Lindsay? Kathleen? Are you girls coming to breakfast? We'll have to leave for church early today so we can practice our song before service," Aunt Elizabeth called up the stairs.

"Oh, no! Our performance! Why? Why do I always get myself into these situations? Quick, Lindsay! Maybe if we brush our hair, the ends won't look so dismal and sad."

Try as they might, nothing could calm the frayed ends, so it was with downcast eyes and blushing

faces that Kathleen and Lindsay slowly walked downstairs to join the family for breakfast. When they entered the room, Kathleen's mama gasped and Kathleen sensed her papa's questioning look. Richard and Robby stifled their giggles at their sisters' astonishing new hairstyles. Kathleen refused to look at anyone. She walked directly to her seat and sat down, fixing her gaze on the stack of steaming biscuits in front of her.

"What's that odd smell?" Grandpa said as he buttered a flapjack. "It reminds me of a medicine the doc gave me two winters ago when I was sick with rheumatism—yet, it smells a jolly bit worse than that."

No one responded. Finally, Mama stood up and broke the long, uncomfortable silence. "Kathleen, there is something I need to talk to you about in the other room before our performance at church—I'm afraid it cannot wait until after breakfast." Mama glanced over at Aunt Elizabeth. An unspoken message passed between them.

"Lindsay, I believe it might not be a bad idea if you and I joined them—it appears we have more preparation than I originally planned."

Kathleen thought she caught a glimmer of a smile in her aunt's eyes, but she could not quite tell. She knew one thing for sure: Lindsay and she had to figure out a way to explain exactly what they had done. Kathleen was not quite out of earshot of the dining room when she heard Robby exclaim, "What happened to their hair?"

"Looks to me like it all got chopped off by the combine," said Richard, "and then they pasted strands of straw to replace it. But it sure does stink a whole lot worse than that."

Kathleen heard the men in the room laughing and recalled her dream of receiving a look of admiration from her father. Instead, she looked terrible and smelled even worse. Her cheeks burned with shame. Lindsay and she must have become used to the smell of the camphor. She should have put another dash of Grandma's rose water in the mixture. Kathleen dearly hoped the smell would wear off before church.

CHAPTER

9

A New Hairdo

Your beauty should not come from outward adornment, such as braided hair and the wearing of gold jewelry and fine clothes. Instead, it should be that of your inner self, the unfading beauty of a gentle and quiet spirit, which is of great worth in God's sight.

1 PETER 3:3–4

Mama, scissors in hand, led the way out of the house and across the lawn. Aunt Elizabeth was at her heels, and Kathleen and Lindsay followed in silence, daring not to ask any questions. When they got to Grandma's kitchen, Mama put a kettle of water on the stove to boil, and Aunt Elizabeth got out the washbasin. After the girls' heads had been thoroughly washed, Mama motioned for them to take one of the stools that sat in the middle of the kitchen floor. She began cutting the frayed ends off Kathleen's hair with swift snips. Kathleen cringed with each cut.

She watched as her beautiful red hair built up on the kitchen floor.

"I should scold both of you for whatever foolishness you've encouraged each other to do, but I gather by the looks on your faces that you have already been punished enough," Aunt Elizabeth chided, but her voice was so sympathetic that it made Kathleen want to cry.

"I can only imagine that this was your idea, Kathleen, so I expect you to do the bulk of explaining," Mama said. "But first, I want you to sit as still as possible with your chin up, so I can salvage what hair I can and make you look halfway respectable before church." Mama put her hand under Kathleen's chin and lifted it until she could see directly into her eyes.

While Kathleen and Lindsay took turns getting their hair cut, they tearfully explained their story and found their mothers to be a bit shocked at the ingredients the girls had used in their curling solution.

"It's no wonder your hair was burned. Camphor is highly flammable and borax is toxic. As to all those other ingredients you decided to add and substitute, I'm surprised there wasn't an explosion!" Mama exclaimed.

"I'm just thankful the whole house was not rendered up in flames," Aunt Elizabeth added. She brushed and then pinned Lindsay's much shorter hairdo back with a bobby pin, trying to keep her

thick bangs out of her eyes. "Let this be a lesson to you girls never to combine any toxic formulas. I know you cannot imagine it right now, but things really could have turned out much worse."

~

True to her aunt's words, Kathleen could not imagine anything being worse than walking into church that Easter morning with her hair all chopped off. She determined right then and there to never again mix dangerous chemicals, and more importantly, she decided that once and for all she had learned the grave importance of humility. She determined to never let her vanity get in the way of good, sound judgment ever again.

"I like your new hairstyle, Kathleen," Bruce said as they walked up the steps to the church.

Kathleen grimaced and kept her eyes on the ground. She was in no mood to be teased.

"No, really, I'm serious. You look nice." Bruce opened the door for her.

"Thank you, Bruce." Kathleen glanced around the open foyer. There were at least twenty people mingling about, but it did not take long for her to notice William standing near the sanctuary door. Lindsay quickly passed by him with her head turned the other direction in an obvious attempt to pretend that something at the other side of the room had caught her attention. William's surprised expression was just as obvious as he stared in shock at the back of Lindsay's mangled hair.

Kathleen was glad that Lindsay had not seen William's face. Poor girl! She was so shy and disliked anything that would bring her extra attention. Now Kathleen had gotten her into this mess. Lindsay's beautiful golden hair was chopped off and fried to a crisp, and William had definitely noticed it. Even though Lindsay had known William all her life and claimed to think of him like one of her brothers, she looked so embarrassed she probably would not dare speak a word to him for months.

Thankfully, the service began before anyone else could say something about the girls' hair. Kathleen scooted into the pew next to Lindsay, keeping her eyes on the floor. She thought she heard some whispering behind her and someone said, "Such a shame."

Dear God, I'm so embarrassed. I know in my head that true beauty is more than my outer appearance. Please help me to know it in my heart too.

"Kathleen," said her mother, "it's time."

Kathleen had prayed all the way to church that the wagon would break down or by some miracle the special music would be cancelled. She'd even pleaded with her mother to have mercy and not have Lindsay and her to accompany them as they sang. But to no avail. Mama said she must face her problem head-on.

When she glanced at Papa, he'd smiled and said it was good for her character.

Grandma seemed to be the only one who understood the agony that the girls were going through. "I understand how awkward you feel having your hair all chopped off. Back in Scotland, when I was a lassie near your age, I couldn't afford a bonnie haircut. One day I got some shears and decided to take matters into me own hands. I needn't say any more. You imagine what I looked like." Grandma Maggie gently brushed a short strand of hair out of Kathleen's face. "Take heart, dearie; it will grow back soon. At least your new hairdo looks cute and spunky. Mine looked so bad I wore my winter cap outdoors and inside for well over a month."

Kathleen appreciated Grandma Maggie's efforts to encourage her, but despite all, she was still self-conscious when it came time for the special music. Kathleen said one last prayer as she and Lindsay rose from their pew and followed their mothers to the front of the church.

"Try to look just above everyone's heads," Kathleen whispered to Lindsay as they took their places at the front of the church. "That way the congregation will think that you're looking at them, but you won't have to look anyone in the eye." Lindsay was so nervous all she could manage in response was a wobbly smile.

Somehow Lindsay and Kathleen were able to focus as they accompanied their mothers' duet, "In the Garden." Both girls managed to avoid making any mistakes, but neither of them could look at the obviously fixed gazes of their family and the whole congregation.

On the way home from church, Kathleen rode with Lindsay, Richard, Robby, and her uncle and aunt in their carriage. The rest of the family rode with Grandpa and Grandma. They were almost home when Uncle John pulled the carriage off the road and turned into the Williamses' drive.

"We'll see you back at the farm." Aunt Elizabeth waved to Kathleen's mama in the other carriage. "We shouldn't be long."

"Take your time. Grandma Maggie and I will get brunch started," Mama said as they passed.

"Where are we going?" Richard leaned out the side of the carriage to get a better look.

"I had an extra smoked ham and thought we would bring it to the Williamses as an Easter gift." Aunt Elizabeth picked up a large basket off the floor and placed it in her lap. Kathleen's heart beat a little faster. Her uncle and aunt, Bruce, Alex, and Mama had all been to visit the Williamses at different times since that awful blizzard several months before. She had wanted to come too, but between school and farm chores there had not been any time.

"Can we get out and play? They have a boy my age, don't they?" Robby bounced excitedly up and down on the leather carriage seat as they pulled into the farmyard.

"Sit still, Robby; you're wrinkling my dress." Lindsay put her hand on her brother's shoulder. Kathleen could see that Lindsay was still struggling with her new hairstyle and did not want to see anyone.

"We'll have to wait and see, Robby. The children are pretty shy; we don't want to make them nervous. When they're ready to play, they will." Uncle John pulled the horse to a stop. "Whoa there, Lightning." His black gelding snorted and stomped impatiently.

Two of the younger Williams girls were scattering feed to the chickens out in the barnyard. Kathleen smiled and waved. When they saw her, they let their aprons fall open, dumping the rest of their feed on the ground. They darted across the yard and disappeared around the back of the house.

"John, should the children wait in the wagon?" Aunt Elizabeth asked as Uncle John took the basket and helped her down.

Kathleen held her breath. She wanted to see their oldest daughter, Sharly, again. They were about the same age and Kathleen desired to know her better.

"Yes, I think that's best for now. We don't want to impose."

Kathleen rested her chin on her hand and sighed. She remembered that the children seemed scared when they rescued them after the snowstorm, but she had figured it was because of the grave conditions they were in. Kathleen wondered why they were still so shy. She was convinced that, given the chance, they could be great friends.

Uncle John knocked on the door, and Aunt Elizabeth waited beside him with basket in hand. Soon, Mr. Williams opened it. He was wearing a clean, pressed pair of overalls and a brown and red checked shirt. Aunt Elizabeth said a few words and handed him the basket. Kathleen strained to hear but could not make out a word. Mrs. Williams came to the door, holding their new baby boy. Kathleen was surprised at how much he had grown since January. Mrs. Williams smiled sweetly but seemed a little uncomfortable. A few more words passed between the two couples. Then Uncle John reached out to shake Mr. Williams' hand. They said good-bye and turned and left.

Kathleen did not even see Sharly. She tried to hide her disappointment. There must be a good reason that her aunt and uncle did not let them go to the door. She would have to trust that they knew best.

Later that evening, back in the solace of Lindsay's room, Kathleen sat on her cousin's bed and stared at her reflection in the mirror. Throughout the day, Kathleen kept forgetting about her short hair. Out of habit, she would try to brush her cowlick back and find it pinned to her head, too short to fall in her face. Or she would walk by a mirror in the parlor, or washroom, and gasp when she saw her reflection. Kathleen wondered why she had ever put the curling concoction in her hair; she always tied it up in rags every night anyway and her curls turned out just fine. But the draw of having extra beautiful tight curls, as the magazine had advertised, and the desire to help Lindsay be something she wasn't, had been too great.

Kathleen's new look was growing on her, but she missed her long hair. "Oh well," she shrugged. "It will grow back."

Jumping up, she remembered her one bright spot in the day, and she was excited to write and tell Lucy about it. She opened the trunk where she kept her stationery and pen.

Dear Lucy,

It's Easter Sunday, and I can scarcely believe it has been nearly three months since I saw you last. If it weren't for all your letters, I know I would not have been able to bear it. I'm so thankful that Dr.

Schmitt feels that your lungs are nearly healed from that terrible bout of pneumonia last January. God is so good! It delights me even more to know that Dr. Schmitt thinks that country air will improve your health . . .

. . . for you see, I've come up with a marvelous plan. Why don't you come and stay at Stonehaven as soon as school lets out? I have already talked to Mama and Papa about it and they think it is a marvelous idea. Papa says that you can ride back with him the next time he goes to Fort Wayne to look for work.

You could stay a week or two or even three . . . I can't wait to show you the adventures of Stonehaven farm life. My grandparents, aunt and uncle, and cousins would love to meet you. They don't get many visitors way out here in the middle of Nowheresville, but they are most hospitable. I can't wait to show you Lindsay's horse, Nellie, and her new filly, Doll. I want you to see the hayloft hideout, the little one-room schoolhouse that I've been attending, the big tire swing, and so many other interesting spots here in my new home away from home.

Oh! I finally saw the Williams family today, at least some of them—from a distance. My aunt and uncle gave them a ham for their Easter Sunday dinner, but they thought it best if we stayed in the wagon. I don't really understand why, but they said something about the children being shy. Anyway, as soon as school lets out, I hope to get to know Sharly better. I don't think she has any friends. Maybe you and I can both get to know her at the same time . . .

Kathleen went on to tell Lucy all about her hair curling disaster and how much harder it seemed to be on Lindsay than it was on her.

I miss you ever so dearly and hope to see you soon.
Your devoted friend,
Kathleen

CHAPTER

10

The Mysterious Meeting in the Woods

God has said, "Never will I leave you; never will I forsake you." . . . The Lord is my helper; I will not be afraid. What can man do to me?

HEBREWS 13:5B–6

Spring was nearly over and everyone at Stonehaven was busy plowing the fields, planting the gardens, and caring for the newly born milk and beef calves, the eight new lambs, and the two litters of piglets. Kathleen enjoyed bottle-feeding the milk calves, and she thought that the newborn Highland beef calves were the cutest animals on the farm. Their furry red hair made them look like little teddy bears, and they were as gentle and cuddly as the baby lambs.

Lucy had not been able to come to the farm yet, but her papa had promised she could as soon as summer came and the night air was no longer cold. Kathleen could not wait.

On this unseasonably cool evening, Kathleen and Robby were responsible for bringing in the cows that had been grazing in the fields and they were having a difficult time finding them.

"I cannot figure out where the cows have gone," said Robby, scanning the hillside. "I don't know why we let them out of the barn during the day only to round them up again at night." Robby dragged his feet in the dirt.

Kathleen could tell he was tired from their long search. "We let them out to find fresh sprigs of grass to munch on so they can produce milk for us to drink." She repeated what Papa had told her when she'd asked the same thing not too long ago. Kathleen tousled Robby's red hair. "If I were a cow, cooped up in the barn all winter long and most of the springtime, I would run as far away as possible, just like they have done. Let's stop and listen awhile and see if we can't hear their cowbells."

They waited for a few minutes, but heard nothing, so they started walking again.

"I still don't see why the cows have to go so far—and off our property too? They always seem to find a hole in the fence." Robby bent down, picked up a stick, and snapped it in two.

"Most likely it's because the snow melted a few weeks ago and it hasn't rained since. That means the

only patches of green grass are along the riverbanks, and even those are few and far between." Kathleen stopped on a high point and surveyed the dark rolling farmland that stretched as far as she could see, broken only by the large trees that grew among the woods near the river and along the streams. "I'm sure we'll find Clover and the other cows soon. Bruce said that they shouldn't be much farther than the riverbed with the large willow, and we passed that a long time ago."

Kathleen surprised herself with how much she had learned about farm life in the past few months. As confident as she sounded though, she wondered if she had misunderstood Bruce's directions. They had been searching for over an hour and dusk had quickly arrived. They had followed several smaller streams that Robby insisted he remembered were where Alex and Bruce always found the cows. But now, as Kathleen looked around at the bare fields on their left and thick brush and tangled vines that lined the stream on their right, it was clear they were much farther from Stonehaven than she had ever been. She was turned around and unsure they would be able to find their way home. Kathleen brushed the thought out of her mind—surely Robby knew the way. He lived here.

"We better hurry. It will be dark soon," Kathleen said, urging Robby to press on.

They had not gone far when Kathleen heard a low moan from somewhere deep within the heavily

wooded grove just ahead. For some strange reason, the noise gave her a cold, eerie feeling.

"Did you hear that?" Kathleen asked.

"It came from over there," said Robby, pointing in the direction of the sound. "One of those cows must have fallen in a ditch or gotten tangled up in something." Robby climbed up out of the creek bank and raced toward the thicket of trees.

Kathleen followed closely behind. The last rays of daylight had grown dim, but inside the woods it looked as dark as night. Robby did not seem to care as he stumbled with blind determination toward where they had last heard the noise.

"I guess you forgot how tired you were?" Kathleen teased as she worked to keep up with him. It wasn't long before they heard the sound a second time. It started as a curiously odd, almost frightening low chant, rising and falling again with a mysterious smoothness that Kathleen could only liken to the surge of a wave. It was the sickest cow she had ever heard. Yet—it sounded more like a human voice than anything. But that wasn't likely. Kathleen decided that her wild imagination was getting the best of her once again. The last time she was startled by a strange noise in the woods, it was only a lost peacock.

By the time they heard the noise again, it was loud and clear, coming from just over the small ridge directly in front of them.

Robby abruptly stopped. "Th-that didn't sound like a c-cow—did it?" Robby stammered just above a whisper.

Kathleen shook her head. Whatever it was, it was straight ahead through the thick underbrush. The tall oak and elm trees cast dark shadows, making it impossible to see. She thought she saw small flickers of light dancing on the branches. Could it be from a lantern or a campfire? Kathleen closed her eyes and opened them again. Surely it was her imagination.

"Robby, what time of year do you get fireflies in Ohio?" Kathleen whispered.

"Not till later. Why?"

"Oh, never mind." Kathleen shifted uneasily. There was no way that the light she was seeing reflected against the treetops could be from fireflies—even if it was the right time of year.

Part of Kathleen wanted to turn around and head for home, but at the same time curiosity burned within her. If the noise was not coming from a cow, which seemed almost impossible at this point, Kathleen would not be satisfied until she knew for sure what it was. Kathleen did not want to run home frightened for no reason, like she had done with Lucy in Kirk's Woods. She forced herself to go on.

"Let's crawl to the top of the ridge." Kathleen dropped to her knees and motioned for Robby to follow.

"Why? You—you don't think there is any danger do you?" His voice shook.

Kathleen realized her heart was racing. She took a deep breath, forcing her nerves to relax.

Dear God, please give me courage and please protect us from harm.

Her short prayer helped. She felt calmer and said with a steady voice, "If I thought we were in danger, I would not be here. Something strange is going on here and my mind will not rest until we figure it out." Kathleen crawled forward—not even taking the time to look back to make sure Robby was following.

They inched their way up the little ridge as quietly as possible. With each passing moment Kathleen's heart beat a little faster and her pulse rose a bit higher. The chanting noise reached a peak about the same time they crested the small incline. This sent a cold, gripping chill up Kathleen's back, and it felt as though her hair was standing up on the back of her neck.

Through the thick trees and underbrush, Kathleen could only occasionally see any details below them. What she was able to make out made her shudder with fright. Deathly looking men—or beings—garbed in long white robes formed a circle in a small clearing. Each held a torch and chanted an eerie tune that rose and fell with the flicker of the flame they held in their hand. Their heads were covered with a white pointed hood, masking any form or face that might hide beneath them.

Robby pressed in closer to Kathleen and grabbed her hand for reassurance. She turned and caught a glimpse of his frightened face as the flickering light cast by one of the torches shone on their hiding place. Quickly, Kathleen put her hand to her lips and motioned for him to keep quiet. Kathleen had no idea what was going on, but whatever it was she knew she did not want to be discovered by these ghostly men.

Kathleen looked back at the scene below, trying to make sense of the whole thing. Abruptly, the chanting stopped, and a large ball of fire rose from the center of the ring. For a moment it was so bright Kathleen feared their hiding place would be seen. The light also gave Kathleen a chance to study these mysterious forms better. Their robes were pure white, with the exception of a round black circle over their hearts. In the center of the circle was a white cross. Their hoods were pure white with two oval slits for eyeholes. Kathleen could not see any faces—just deep black holes. She shuddered at the thought of what sort of man, or being, might be hiding behind such a mask. Kathleen closed her eyes and prayed silently.

Dear Lord, please protect us—please don't let us be caught and help us to get home safely.

Kathleen opened her eyes. The ball of fire burned down, revealing the solitary outline of a large, burning

cross. Kathleen gasped and quickly placed her hand over her mouth. The chanting started again. Kathleen slowly and quietly eased her way back down the embankment, eager to be out of sight. She had seen enough. Whatever was going on, Kathleen knew it was wrong. She could feel a sort of heaviness in her spirit and ache in her heart that she had never sensed before. She would not feel safe or peaceful until she and Robby had put a good distance between themselves and the wicked-looking men below.

CHAPTER 11

Friend or Foe?

The LORD *is near to all who call on him, to all who call on him in truth. He fulfills the desires of those who fear him; he hears their cry and saves them.*

PSALM 145:18–19

Kathleen and Robby tore through the brush. Neither of them dared speak or even look back until they were completely out of the woods and positive they were well out of earshot. The last glimmer of sunset had disappeared by the time they reached the creek, and the moon had already risen in the sky.

"Who were those men?" asked Robby between deep gulps of air.

"I don't know," said Kathleen. "You've never seen them before?" Despite being out of breath, Kathleen's words tumbled over each other in the same fashion that Robby and she had just stumbled out of the woods. She tried to keep her tone calm and even, but she could not get the mysteriously wicked, eerie sight out of her mind. The torches they carried accentuated the dark eyeholes cut in their odd-shaped pointed hoods. She hoped that the strange people had not spotted them.

"Never." Robby's eyes were as round as silver dollars. "That was the scariest thing I ever saw in my whole life!"

"I don't know what was going on back there, but the one thing I do know is that those men were up to no good." Kathleen slowed to a walk. She looked around. The dark woods were at their backs and they were in a gully near the creek.

"Good thing the moon is full tonight, or we would never find our way back. Do you know where we are?"

"I—I don't know," Robby said hopelessly.

"I thought you said that you had followed this creek before with Alex and Bruce," Kathleen said. She searched the horizon for any sign of light or life—but all she saw in the moonlight was the outline of dark hills.

"I did. At least I thought I knew the way, but then when we got to the edge of those woods back there, I realized that I've never seen them before. I was about to tell you that when we heard the noise." Robby glanced back toward the foreboding woods and shivered.

"Robby, look." Kathleen pointed to a large knoll just ahead of them. "Let's climb up to that high point. Maybe from there we'll be able to see lights from a farmhouse window." Kathleen couldn't wait to see real people again just to confirm to herself that what they'd just witnessed was real and not a bad dream. She started up the muddy bank, ignoring the fact that she was about to lose a shoe in the sludge. By the time she reached the top, her shoe was long gone—buried in a deep, watery footprint somewhere in the shadowy moonlight that crept through the trees along the stream bank. She hardly missed it though. After all, those men might be following them even now. Their own lives were far more important than a shoe.

"There! Way across the field, did you see that light flicker?" Robby shouted. Just then the loud crack of a snapping branch sounded from somewhere behind them.

"Shhh." Kathleen's heart quickened. "I think we're being followed." The light Robby spoke of did little to ease her mind. In the distant horizon, a faint flicker appeared one moment and then disappeared the next. "I see—it must be someone carrying a lantern. Maybe whoever it is can direct us back to home," Kathleen whispered.

They raced across a newly plowed field full of clumps of sod toward the light, but no matter how much ground they covered, the light seemed to be just as far away—if not a little farther. Kathleen tried to keep Robby's courage up, but she knew he was tired and hungry. Robby tripped on a clod of dirt and fell face-first to the ground. At the same time, the brave,

tough front that her eight-year-old cousin had tried to hold up came tumbling down too.

"I—I can't go on. I'm hungry and I want my m-ma," he sobbed.

Kathleen knelt and put her arms around him. "We will be fine, Robby. We have to find our way sooner or later—Stonehaven could be just beyond that little rise." Kathleen pointed to a small hill to the side of them that she could see in the moonlight. She sighed heavily. She wished it was. What were they going to do? They could not stay out here all night in their chilled and wet condition—they would surely catch a cold.

Kathleen shuddered at the thought. It was not until then that Kathleen noticed how cold and sore her bare foot was. Kathleen felt a little nudging deep within her heart, and she realized that she had been trying to find her way in the dark all on her own.

She had completely forgotten to pray and ask her Heavenly Father to direct their steps. Papa often talked about running the race of life. This must be what he was talking about. He said there would be times in life when she might feel all alone in a deep valley, not sure which way to turn, with nights growing so cold and dark that she might even stumble. At those times God would still be right there—even if the trial was so dark that she couldn't see Him.

"Robby, we've forgotten something really important," Kathleen said out loud.

Robby stopped sobbing. "What?" He rubbed his eyes.

"We need to pray." Kathleen took his hand. Robby and she closed their eyes, and Kathleen asked God to lead them home. Before she said amen, she heard a noise approaching. It sounded like a car motor. Kathleen opened her eyes and saw car lights coming their way. She and Robby were less than a hundred feet from a country road.

"Look, Kathleen! God answered our prayer." Robby jumped up and rushed toward the road.

"Wait up! Don't get run over!" Kathleen could scarcely contain her emotions. She was excited, relieved, and concerned all at the same time. After all, she had no way of knowing who was driving the car, and in light of what they'd just witnessed she wasn't sure she could trust a stranger.

They made it to the road just before the car got to them. Kathleen waved her arms desperately. For one lovely second she thought the car was slowing, but her hopes were dashed as it drove right past.

"Now what are we going to do?" Robby cried pitifully as he stared at its dimming taillights.

"Look! The car. It's stopping and backing up." Kathleen jumped up and down in her excitement.

The man inside rolled his window down. Kathleen noticed a rather large dog practically sitting in his lap. Something about the man seemed familiar, but she

couldn't quite place it in the dim light. His weathered face was covered slightly by gray whiskers, and his hair was in need of a good trimming and looked as if it hadn't been washed in weeks.

"You kids need a lift? What are you doing way out here after dark without a lantern anyway?" The man looked down at their muddy, torn clothing.

"Well, sir, my cousin and I were looking for our cows and we lost our way. We live at Stonehaven, the McKenzie farm—do you happen to know where that is?" Kathleen asked anxiously.

"McKenzie, did you say? I should have known . . . I suppose giving you two a ride would be the only neighborly thing to do." The man was clearly irritated. "Climb on in."

Kathleen wondered what they could have done to upset him or why he thought he should have recognized them. But she was relieved he was familiar with her family.

"Do you know how far it is to Stonehaven, sir?" Kathleen asked as Robby and she climbed in the backseat.

" 'Bout four miles from here—only two as the crow flies," the man mumbled.

Two miles? Kathleen was surprised that she and Robby had gotten so far away from home. In the dark, it would've taken them forever to travel that far.

Hoping to ease the peculiar tension she felt radiating from the man, Kathleen said, "You must live around here. I'm new here. My family and I are visiting at my relatives' farm. We come from Fort Wayne. Thank you for helping us Mr.—I guess I don't know your name, sir. I believe we have never met." Kathleen knew she was talking too much, just as she always did when she was nervous.

"You are only right about one thing—you definitely *are* new in the area, and evidently prone to mischief. However, we have met before. If I'm not mistaken, you are Kathleen, known far and wide for your excellent marksmanship. I am Mr. Johnston. This is my dog." He patted him on the head. "You're already well acquainted with him. His name's Bruiser."

Kathleen felt her mouth drop open. Bruiser was the name of the dog she'd accidentally shot last winter. This had to be his mean owner, the one she'd apologized to at the risk of her own life.

"Ah, Mr. Johnston. I didn't recognize you in the dark. How is Bruiser?" Her mouth felt dry and she suddenly wondered if she and Robby were in for a tongue lashing.

"His wound healed well enough, I guess. Good thing I'm not a man to hold a grudge, or I would have had a mind to just leave the both of you out in the cold." Mr. Johnston's tone grew edgier by the second.

Kathleen swallowed. From what Bruce and Alex had said, Mr. Johnston was mean enough to carry out his threat. "I'm so glad to see your dog is okay." Kathleen leaned forward to scratch the old dog behind the ears. Bruiser stood up on the seat and eagerly wagged his tail, hitting his master in the face.

"Sit." Mr. Johnston shouted and shoved the dog to the side of the car.

Kathleen winced at the tone of his voice. "I—I never meant to shoot your dog, Mr. Johnston. You can imagine the utter horror I felt when I learned what I had done."

"Horror seems like a strong word, but enough about that. Now tell me again, why were you two out roaming around after dark? And I want to know where you have been wandering," he said in a dry, suspicious tone.

Robby squirmed in the seat next to Kathleen. She knew that Mr. Johnston's rough voice was scaring him too.

The shock and embarrassment of riding with Mr. Johnston was disconcerting enough, but there was something in the man's voice that made Kathleen especially uneasy.

Why was he so concerned about them being out after dark? He definitely did not appear to be the type of man that cared much about anything other than himself. Kathleen also wondered why he seemed so curious, almost suspicious of where they had been . . . as if they were up to some sort of mischief. Unless he had something to hide? Something white stuffed under the front seat caught her eye.

"We got lost," said Robby. "Then, we thought we heard a noise—"

Kathleen grabbed Robby's leg and pointed at the white object. It was a bundle of material that resembled that used on the long robes they had just seen an hour before.

Robby's eyes grew wide.

"What sort of noise—where did you say you heard it coming from?" Mr. Johnston asked, glancing in the backseat.

Now Kathleen was convinced he was hiding something and it had to do with that awful ceremony or ritual they had stumbled upon. Kathleen's heart beat hard within her chest. Her mind raced. She must alter his questioning, but how?

"At first we thought it was one of our cows, but it sounded more like an old coyote. Isn't that right, Robby?" She prodded him with her elbow.

"Yeah, a coyote." He snuggled up next to her, a quivering mass of fear. Kathleen hoped Mr. Johnston wouldn't notice. She tried to make her voice sound as normal as possible. The last thing she wanted to do was raise his suspicions.

"We never did find our cows. We crawled through a hole in the fence and searched along the river. We

eventually followed a stream. We were looking for grassy areas where they might be feeding. Finally we thought we heard the cows' low mooing, but unfortunately, we never did find them and kept wandering until well after the sun had gone down. By then we were so turned around," Kathleen threw her arms up in the air, "we didn't know which way to go." She giggled, but it sounded more like a whimper. She'd never been very good at acting. "Then we saw a light flashing way across that field where you picked us up. Right, Robby?"

"R-Right," his voice quaked. Kathleen thought she heard his teeth chattering.

"We ran toward it, but never did catch up. It just seemed to get farther away—almost like we were chasing a mirage. We were about to lose all hope when we decided that we should pray and ask God to help us. That's when you came."

Kathleen took a deep breath. She tried to string the story out as long as possible, hoping to either satisfy Mr. Johnston's curiosity or get home before he could ask any more prying questions. She peered out the window, looking for any sign of Stonehaven, only to find black, foreboding fields staring back at her as far as the moonlight allowed her to see.

"Hmm. Sounds innocent enough. You had better mind your own business and not go poking around after dark like that. You might stumble into more trouble than you care to think. The countryside is a dangerous place at night." Mr. Johnston sounded even more agitated than before.

Much to Kathleen's relief, the rest of the ride was silent. When they finally turned into their barnyard, Robby still had his eyes riveted on the white robe.

"Thank you, Mr. Johnston. I don't know what we would have done if you had not come along. You were an answer to our prayers." Kathleen jumped to the ground and winced as her bare foot landed on the cold dirt. She was so anxious to be free from Mr. Johnston's presence that she forgot all about her missing shoe. But now she felt the full effect of running without it. She must have cut her foot on a sharp rock or perhaps on one of the tangled vines and thorn bushes that grew along the stream.

"Just stay away from the woods and mind your own business," Mr. Johnston grumbled.

"Yes, sir, we will st-stay far away, sir," Robby stammered.

Kathleen shuddered at his threat. She knew he was deadly serious. Whatever it was that they were doing back in the woods, he appeared determined to keep it a secret.

Kathleen took Robby's hand and rushed up the stairs to the farmhouse.

Mama and Grandma Maggie met Kathleen and Robby at the front door.

"Thank heaven you are safe." Mama opened her arms and hugged both Kathleen and Robby. "We've been awfully worried—Alex is out looking for you now."

Grandma Maggie peered out the door at the car driving out of the farmyard. "Who's the kind neighbor that brought you home, lass?"

"Mr. Johnston." Kathleen squeezed Grandma Maggie's hand. "It is sure good to be home."

"Kathleen. What happened—where is your shoe and stocking?" Mama asked as she looked at Kathleen's dirty bare foot and soiled dress.

Robby looked up from the floor where he was taking off his muddy shoe. "She lost it in the mud near the stream when we were running away from the scary men dressed in white."

"Who were you running from? Were you hurt?" Mama brushed Kathleen's tangled hair out of her eyes and then found a small dishpan, which she used to clean Kathleen's dirty foot.

"Don't worry, Mama; we are both fine. It is a long story—one that Papa needs to hear too."

"Papa's at the dinner table; we had just sat down when I heard the car pull up," Mama said, as she dried Kathleen's foot and found her another pair of warm socks and shoes.

"Come, you can tell all while we eat." Grandma Maggie put one arm around Kathleen and the other around Robby. "You two must be starved."

Kathleen suddenly felt famished.

~

After Kathleen and Robby finished their story, Alex returned, and then the family pelted them with questions.

"Did they really burn a cross?" Bruce asked as he cut off a piece of venison.

"I'm afraid so," Kathleen nodded soberly.

"Did you get a good look at any of their faces? Could you recognize one of them if you were to see them again?" asked Aunt Elizabeth, twisting and twirling a strand of her blonde hair, which she always did when she was deep in thought or perturbed.

"We couldn't see anything but white robes with dark holes where their eyes should be." Kathleen took a bite of mashed potatoes.

"Are you sure the white robe you saw in Mr. Johnston's car was the same as the ones that you saw the men wearing in the woods?" Bruce looked from Robby to Kathleen.

"No, I can't say for certain—it was rolled up and stuffed under the driver's seat. But from what I could see, it looked a whole lot like what Kathleen and I saw those men wearing." Robby's eyes were still as large as they had been the moment he spied the suspicious white robe in the car.

"Kathleen, what do you think?" Uncle John asked. "I sure would hate to believe that our neighbor—even if he does live a few farms away—would be involved in such a radical, ungodly movement as the Ku Klux Klan." The concerned furrows on Uncle John's brow deepened.

Kathleen remembered reading something about the KKK in history class but had no idea that such groups still existed, especially up North. She thought that the KKK only survived in the Deep South near the farms they called plantations.

She looked at the concerned faces of her family and knew she had to give as accurate an answer as she could. "With the way Mr. Johnston was behaving so oddly and his strange questions about where we'd been and the white robe in his car, I'm afraid the only conclusion I can come to is that he was most definitely involved in the ritual that we stumbled upon." Kathleen tried to sound as brave as she could, but every time she looked at her mother's and Aunt Elizabeth's worried faces, she wanted to break down in tears. Now that she was in the warmth and safety of home, surrounded by those she loved, Kathleen realized how frightened and alone she had felt moments before.

"That possibility is not so far-fetched," said Papa. He took another slice of homemade bread and lathered it with fresh butter. "Just the other day I was reading an article by a man who has researched the modern Klan. I had hoped that the movement was a part of our country's past, but the author claimed the number of members involved today has reached an all-time record high." Papa shook his head in dismay. "I did not believe it at the time, but the article said that the KKK had spread as far north as Indiana. I guess I have no choice now but to believe it."

"What is the KKK anyway? Are they dangerous?" Lindsay had barely eaten a bite on her plate.

"The Ku Klux Klan is a group of people who have a prejudiced political agenda," Grandpa said. "The worst part is they try to spiritualize the whole thing. But you can trust me when I say there is nothing biblical or God-honoring about it." Grandpa slammed his hand down on the table. "Basically, they are trying to justify their own prejudices and desire for power by saying they base their convictions on biblical principles and claim that they are trying to protect Christianity in America. However, nothing could be further from the truth!"

"Grandpa is right." Papa stood and paced the floor as he talked. "From what I've read they are a gang of men trying to justify their craving for power by threatening to eliminate people that don't fit into their political views."

"Sometimes they actually do it," added Grandpa.

Richard and Robby gasped and Lindsay gave a little cry.

"Now Grandpa," said Grandma Maggie, "don't frighten the children."

"Unfortunately, they call themselves Christians, but the Bible says that you will know other Christians by their good fruit, and by those standards, the KKK is terribly wicked."

"Papa, what do you mean when you say they threaten, or e—eliminate people that don't match up to their views?" Kathleen asked. She replayed the whole eerie scene of the men dressed as ghosts chanting around the fire. A chill tingled up her spine. Papa must have read the fear in her eyes.

"There is nothing for us to worry about because we happen to be white, Protestant Americans. Around these parts you are in the most danger if you are Catholic, Jewish, or Negro." Papa's hand clenched the back of his dining room chair so hard that his knuckles turned white. "It infuriates me that they even call themselves Christians. God loves us all equally—no matter what our color or creed. He calls us to love equally too and to draw those who do not know Christ to Him through our love—not through fear, intimidation, and hate. In fact, almost all of the KKK's actions and creed are exactly opposed to Christianity, yet they claim to serve God."

Kathleen saw her grandma, grandpa, aunt, and uncle all nodding their heads in agreement. She could see anger and determination on Alex and Bruce's

faces. She knew that her family was in agreement on this issue.

"James," said Grandpa, "I think you should go to town first thing in the morning and a pay a visit to Sheriff Ratcliff. He needs to know there might be serious trouble brewing."

Kathleen thought about the black family who had recently moved up north from Alabama.

"What about the Williamses? Are they in danger?" Kathleen asked.

"I'm afraid they could be," Papa said. "We best warn them."

"We'll have to put forth an even greater effort to make them feel welcome in our community now that we know there are folks around that have, no doubt, been far from neighborly," Uncle John said.

"Yes, dear, I do agree," Aunt Elizabeth said, speaking up for the first time. "I think Lindsay and I will stop by tomorrow and see how their kitchen garden is coming. Maybe we can give them a few tips on planting vegetables here in Ohio. The climate is so different from the South."

"I would love to go with you!" Kathleen said. She thought back to the scared look on their oldest daughter Sharly's face when Kathleen helped rescue them after the blizzard. Perhaps Sharly hadn't been afraid of being buried beneath the snow in their farmhouse, but had been frightened of Kathleen because she was white. Was that why the Williamses had not been to the county schoolhouse—because they thought they would not be accepted? What an awful thought! Maybe some in the South thought like that—and it looked like some folks up North did too—but the McKenzie family never had and they never would.

That night Kathleen lay in bed awake. She thought a lot about Sharly and her family. She hoped their families would become friends. The Williamses all seemed so kind and caring, and she wanted them to feel the love she had for them in her heart. Kathleen also thought a lot about Lucy. She hoped that Lucy could come and visit the farm soon. Lucy had written several times since Easter but never in response to Kathleen's invitation. Now she wondered if Lucy had even gotten that letter. Kathleen decided to write another note to invite her again. Besides, so much had happened that day that Kathleen wanted to tell Lucy. She knew she would not be able to sleep until all her thoughts were written on paper.

Kathleen slipped out of bed. She felt her way through the darkness to the nightstand on Lindsay's side of the bed and carefully lit the lantern. Kathleen quickly took out her spare paper and pen from the travel trunk at the foot of the bed and hurried to the desk. The ink flowed rapidly as she wrote to Lucy telling her how much she hoped that she could come to Stonehaven soon and then all about the disconcerting ritual Robby and she had encountered. Kathleen poured out her thoughts and concerns about the Ku Klux Klan and her apprehensions for the Williams family's safety. As she wrote, visions of the awful ritual Robby and she had witnessed that night flashed before her. Kathleen imagined the great wickedness such men might be capable of. A cold feeling raced up her spine and she shuddered.

Dear Lord, please protect Sharly and her family. Please help them know that we are their friends and want to help, not harm them.

Will the KKK strike the peaceful farming community?
Could the Williams family be in danger?
If so, how can Kathleen help?

Find out in:

KATHLEEN'S ENDURING FAITH

Book Four

A Life of Faith: Kathleen McKenzie Series

Book One	—Kathleen's Shaken Dreams	ISBN: 978-1-928749-25-7
Book Two	—Kathleen's Unforgettable Winter	ISBN: 978-1-928749-26-4
Book Three	—Kathleen's Abiding Hope	ISBN: 978-1-928749-27-1
Book Four	—Kathleen's Enduring Faith	ISBN: 978-1-928749-28-8

For more information or a free catalog, call 1-800-840-2641 or write to:

Mission City Press at 202 Second Ave. South,
Franklin, Tennessee 37064
or visit our Web Site at

www.alifeoffaith.com

ABOUT THE AUTHOR

Author Tracy Leininger Craven is known for capturing the stories of real-life Christian heroines from America's past in historical fiction books. She is the author of many titles, including:

- **Alone Yet Not Alone**
  The Story of Barbara and Regina Leininger
- **Unfading Beauty**
  The Story of Dolley Madison
- **The Land Beyond the Setting Sun**
  The Story of Sacagawea
- **Nothing Can Separate Us**
  The Story of Nan Harper
- **A Light Kindled**
  The Story of Priscilla Mullins
- **Our Flag Was Still There**
  The Story of the Star-Spangled Banner

Tracy Leininger Craven loves history and the people whose lives have left an indelible impression on our country's heritage. She is also inspired by the testimony of God's faithfulness through seemingly impossible circumstances. Her stories of real people come alive and serve to mentor and inspire a new generation of readers.

Tracy, her husband David, and their daughters Elaina Hope and Evangelina Lilly live in the beautiful Texas Hill Country.

For more information, visit www.hisseasons.com or call (210) 490-2101.

Meet the Other *A Life of Faith* Heroines and Discover Their Intriguing Adventures!

Elsie Dinsmore
Elsie's Endless Wait

Millie Keith
Millie's Unsettled Season

Violet Travilla
Violet's Hidden Doubts

Laylie Colbert
Laylie's Daring Quest